SACRED SOULS

ZARA HOFFMAN

Sacred Souls.
Copyright © 2021 Zara Hoffman.
Sacred Souls/Zara Hoffman – 1st ed.
ISBN 978-0-9896294-9-2

Book Cover Design ©2017 White Rabbit Book Design

To Regina and Maria:
Your kindness throughout my author journey warms my heart.

TRIGGER WARNING

Please be aware that this book involves kidnapping and sexual attraction between the prisoner and captor.

If this is triggering for you, please take care of your mental health and skip this book.

This book also includes an episode of physical torture and sexual assault in **Chapter 28***, so please be aware this book may be more upsetting than the previous ones in this trilogy.*

We are bits of stellar matter that got cold by accident, bits of star gone wrong.

SIR ARTHUR EDDINGTON

1

KNOX

KNOX SUPPRESSED a smile as he was ushered across the base into the building where Trohm had been kept.

They didn't know he'd been there before but knowing that his mole had already escaped, he wondered what they were thinking. Not even they could be stupid enough to think that a failed system would work on its second try. At least, not without any improvements and the only thing they could tweak would be the metal—opting for the strongest one on Earth. He doubted they could get it so quickly and implement it in the short time between Trohm's escape and his capture.

The guards didn't say anything as they led him through the front doors, across the lobby, and down the stairs leading to the basement. They were being quite reckless. He could have easily pushed one down the stairs and knocked the other with a simple head-butt.

The only reason these men weren't dead was that he had no interest in becoming a murderer.

The men used a key to unlock a special door and pushed him through, bringing him to the other side of the glass barrier.

Knox let himself be pushed into the metal chair and chuckled when they tied chains around his chest, securing him to the chair. While they were busy pulling the chains tight, he flicked listening devices from his armor's gauntlets onto each guard.

It wasn't a perfect solution since humans did not only wear one outfit but it was still better to have an imperfect advantage than none at all. In addition to the listening devices Zeph had already planted, he should be able to hear almost anything happening on the base in one way or another.

The guards were completely unaware of the devices and turned their attention to chaining his legs together before snapping the seat's metal cuffs around his wrists and ankles.

The chains were cool and heavy, but not particularly uncomfortable. If he wanted to break out, he could yank his arms up until they broke from the manacles and then break the chain that bound him and kick off the rest of the shackles.

Knox could imagine Verity's reaction if she saw him now that he was restrained for a change. And he remembered her subtle but shocked reaction to his insinuation during their first meeting that he tied up his lovers. It was the truth but it wasn't a requirement for him. Arfilmea had never wanted to try it but some of his past liaisons definitely involved bondage.

He wondered if Verity would be amenable to the suggestion. When the time came, he couldn't wait to ask her.

But his increasingly overwhelming desire for her was what had gotten him in this situation. Had he realized it were a trap, he would have also done what Zeph hadn't gotten a chance to— attach a listening device to her so he could be with her throughout her day even while they were physically apart.

And though he had no doubt she was capable of luring him into a trap if she really put her mind to it, he had a sneaking suspicion that it hadn't been her idea.

Knox was still trying to figure out how she had found his location but even if someone had tipped her off, he refused to believe that she'd take the time to enlist her father's military force rather than just confronting him on her own. Fearlessly diving head-first into the situation was much more her style based on how she'd acted on his ship.

Her attempt at lulling him into submission during their last meal together was proof that she wasn't one to come excessively armed to a situation, preferring to do things mostly on her own. He had deduced her plan not only from the complete change in attitude she'd exhibited by asking him to dinner for the first time, instead of waiting for him to extend an invitation, but also from decoding her secret message to her accomplice. Her plan had involved working with her captain, but she had taken on arguably the harder and more important task whereas the captain had merely thought he had escaped with another prisoner and met her at the pods. Knox had intentionally told his guards to leave the hangar exposed.

But Verity was also the kind of person to intelligently assess a situation as it unfolded so perhaps she had decided to act out of character to keep him off-balance. It was possible she was utilizing the advantages available to her on her home planet to compensate for being on her own in space but it didn't sit right with him.

Knox would ask her about it when he got the chance but he didn't expect a straight answer from her on the topic. Drawing it out of her would be part of the fun, and maybe it would help him understand where he stood with her.

The guards left, and Knox listened to their footsteps through the wall. When they appeared on the other side of the glass, he saw them nervously glance at him before they vacated the hallway.

Now would be the perfect time to break free if that was his plan but Knox knew the humans would be more likely to let slip information if they thought they had already won. Excessive and misplaced pride was always an easy fault to exploit.

If he had to guess, he supposed Verity believed that's what

she'd been doing during their last meal together. But his pride had never been excessive nor misplaced. His pride was always well-earned, and if he ever started straying towards egotistical narcissism, he could rely on Aerue to politely bring him back down.

After confirming he was truly alone in the basement, Knox opened a communication to Dr. Mak'en.

"Your Majesty," she greeted. "How may I serve you?"

"Please continue the experiment in my absence and keep me apprised of the results."

She nodded, then disappeared as the connection closed. He didn't want to keep it open longer than necessary. It would deplete his armor's power and he needed the stored energy if the humans were going to leave him underground for the duration of his stay.

Knox had soaked in enough sun while at Zeph's home to normally last a month but without any access to food, his time-frame was almost halved. He would leave before that became an issue but he wasn't going to be careless.

His reverie was interrupted by the sound of a visitor arriving.

A few moments passed before a uniformed man entered. He strode very quickly towards the glass barrier.

Knox tilted his head and examined the man. Interesting that he wasn't afraid at all after Trohm had already proven this man-made prison was insufficient to hold him.

Knox leaned back in the seat, almost relaxing into the cool metal material. The hard edges weren't as comfortable as his throne but it was't as bad as he was sure the humans assumed it would be. He could imagine the general taking joy in assuming he was sitting in constant pain. Just another tidbit he'd be keeping to himself.

He raised his eyebrows and waited for the first question. This should be interesting.

2

VERITY

"WHAT THE HELL were you thinking, Verity?" her father bellowed the moment the front door closed behind them, safely ensconcing them in their home again.

"I was thinking that I was going to confront Harrison and Ben's killer."

"And your kidnapper. Without backup! I thought I raised you better than that."

"I'm not a child!"

"You're certainly acting like one. Impulsive to the extreme, no care for your own safety—"

"You could have warned me you were going to send in STFs. They could've shot me!"

"If you had warned me about *your* plan, we could have coordinated. As it was, I sent them in for your protection. They never would have injured you, and you know that. They're trained and disciplined." He emphasized the last word.

She didn't have a rejoinder. And she supposed she should be glad things had turned out as they did. She had been about to kiss Knox again. And time had already proven she didn't think clearly when that happened.

And if any of the STFs had reported they'd captured Knox while he was in the middle of kissing her, she had no doubt her father would say screw national security and kill the alien king instead.

"Okay, we have him. What now?" she asked.

"We interrogate him."

"And?"

"He can't hurt you anymore."

"Trohm wasn't held in that cell. What makes you think Knox won't be out before they finish locking him in?"

"We've taken extra precautions."

Verity doubted they'd be any more effective than the titanium chair had been. But she wasn't about to poke the bear that was her father right now.

She'd been doing it enough since her return and that had been without having Knox within kissing—or punching—distance.

But she hadn't nearly gotten enough time with him before her father's meddling had broken them up. "Can I talk to him?" she asked, already bracing herself for her father's negative reaction.

"No." The word was firm but not especially loud.

She'd expected shouting.

"He might open up to me."

"You're not to approach him again."

"Then can I talk to him through a speaker or something? Trohm didn't say anything until I talked to him and Knox has even more control than him."

"And you think Trohm really opened to you? How do you know they weren't just lying to you this whole time? You're being naive to think that they're being honest with you."

"What do we have to lose—if I'm talking to him from afar?" She tacked on the clarification before he could point out the obvious danger of Knox kidnapping her again if she were close enough for him to do so.

She was still convinced it was a possibility but if she told her father that, she'd probably never be able to leave her room until she was an old lady. By then, she'd probably be too old to get down the stairs to the front door.

Her father stared at her, a frown pulling his mouth down and a line creasing his forehead. If he kept that up, he'd start looking older than he was. Though, as an intimidating General, she supposed it could be seen as a benefit.

She resisted the urge to tap her foot while she waited for his verdict. It would only piss him off.

"Okay," her father finally conceded. "You can watch recordings from the office here. And that's it."

He pulled his phone out of his pocket and dialed. "Cyber, send Mr. Powell over ASAP."

She heard the voice on the other side say, "He's not here, sir. He's taken some personal time off," as clearly if they were in the same room.

"Then send someone else. I need the security cameras from Building Zulu to my home office."

"Yes, sir."

Her father hung up without another word to the person.

"I'm assigning extra guards to surround the house at all times and a second guard to help McDonald. They'll be swapping in and out, and you'll barely notice them. No manipulating them, Verity. I mean it."

"I understand," she answered but made no verbal promise. It was a small loophole but she had a feeling it would be necessary. He luckily didn't call her on it.

Her father was dialing again, already thinking of other things. "Get Special Agent Kaur here. I'll meet him at the gate."

"Yes, sir," his assistant said.

Verity made a face at the name, and her father said, "You don't have to see him now. But I have a feeling he'll want another meeting after interrogating the prisoner."

Joy.

"How long will you be gone this time?" she asked.

"Unknown. You can call my assistant for food and don't worry about ordering for me."

She nodded. "What about seeing Dr. Hudson now? Am I still stuck here for everything?"

Her father gave it a brief moment of consideration before he said, "As long as you have multiple guards with you, I don't see why that would be an issue. But you'll have to use another office today. I'll have my assistant prepare another room for you."

He dropped a quick kiss to the top of her head, rendering her momentarily speechless and frozen at the uncharacteristically tender gesture.

He was already out the door before she regained her senses.

McDonald walked in from the security room and noted her dazed appearance.

"You okay?"

She turned toward him and smiled. "Yeah. Fine." Well, as fine as she could be with her life still being held in the frustratingly strong and attractive hands of a certain alien king.

VERITY WALKED through the security scanner and proceeded to the elevator bank without an extra search this time.

She waited for McDonald and Flynn—her current second guard—to be cleared for entrance. Her father clearly wasn't taking any chances since Tristan had been revealed to be the alien Trohm.

Once they had joined, she used the iris scanner to enter the elevator and selected the third floor. The three of them were silent as they zoomed upward and her shadows didn't utter a word when she greeted Dr. Hudson in the waiting room.

Her father's assistant met them at the door leading to the different offices and ushered them into one of the conference rooms in the opposite direction of her father's office.

Dr. Hudson didn't ask about the change of location or comment on McDonald and Flynn's going into the room before them.

They were clearing it for security threats and quickly finished their check. Once McDonald nodded at her, she walked inside. Dr. Hudson followed her and closed the door.

Verity activated the lock and sat down at the center of the table. It was too big to make sitting at the head comfortable for her. It felt too formal, especially with it being only her and Dr. Hudson.

She watched as the woman pulled out her notebook and pen, and waited. She wasn't sure how to start but after what had happened, she felt like she needed a session to process it. When your captor is captured... that's what was supposed to happen —right?

"How are you feeling today, Verity?"

"Strange."

Dr. Hudson waited for her to elaborate.

"Well, my kidnapper was caught."

"Really?"

Verity nodded but didn't offer any extra explanation. If she was pressed, she could pull the classified card but hoped she wouldn't have to. Because hearing something was "classified" naturally only made people more curious. Curiosity may have killed the cat but that couldn't kill the feeling itself.

"And you feel strange after hearing that news?"

"I can't explain it, really."

The psychiatrist waited her out.

"It's not that I'm not glad," she started. It's not like she had Stockholm syndrome. "but I just—I don't know—"

"Don't feel safe yet?"

She nodded.

"Do you believe he's still a danger to you or have you merely not had time to recognize the new reality of him no longer being a threat?"

Definitely the former. Even if he was telling the truth about not killing Harrison and Ben, she was certain he could have done so easily. And any other alien, for that matter. And based on how much stronger the alien restraints had been on her, she doubted her father's earth ones were truly effective. Knox was only in custody because he wasn't fighting back.

"The first one," she said. "Am I being paranoid?" She knew the real answer was no but she had a feeling her psychiatrist might disagree with her because she only had a partial picture of the situation.

"Remember when you froze during fight training?"

Hello, non-sequitur.

"Yeah..."

"Were you in any real danger at that moment?"

"No."

"But your mind made you believe you were, based on your body's memories."

"I don't get how that relates to this. That was a trigger. Doesn't it make sense that I'd react that way?"

"Yes. Completely normal. But that's not the comparison I'm trying to draw here, Verity. My point is that in that situation, and perhaps this one, your trauma memory is trying to protect you from the same or worse happening again. It takes time for your mind to readjust to your safe reality and let you live with that reassurance."

"Oh." That made sense. Generally, of course. But maybe if they ever found a way to truly neutralize Knox as a threat, she'd be feeling the same way. If that time ever came, at least she would be able to take comfort in knowing there was a light at the end of the tunnel.

Now, though, the dark fear extended too far out to see anything else.

3

KNOX

KNOX HEARD the cameras switch back on. He wasn't particularly sure when they had been switched off but he supposed there hadn't been any point for the humans to continue recording an empty cell once Trohm had escaped.

He brought up the star map again, this time in the ultraviolet light spectrum so the humans wouldn't be able to see it, and noted how the Vruxilian ships not only encircled his own but were now touching it. Perhaps they were all docked, and the siege had moved onto the next stage.

He pulled up a communication to Aerue after whispering his name in a sub-audible frequency, but didn't get an answer. He tried twice more, but to no avail.

Was his friend in danger, or was he merely being smart by not answering his calls to avoid Eiz'm's attention? Either way, Knox needed more information. Trohm and Zeph wouldn't have yet reached the ship but once they had, they would contact them for a report.

Knox scanned his surroundings again for the millionth time. Without anything better to do, it was his only form of intellectual stimulation. He'd already spotted the cameras before he was even a prisoner but now he was seeing the small cracks from where the first glass barrier had shattered and the small warping of the new one.

Glass was a very interesting substance. His grandfather hadn't seen reason to use much of the substance since he considered it weak but his father had been able to appreciate it more. Appearing solid, technically a liquid, and beautiful with its imperfections. And it came in all varying types.

Earth seemed to be ahead of them in this one aspect: admiring the material to the point of making art with it through color and shape, sometimes combining the two into sculptures rather than two-dimensional images found in their religious institutions.

He wished Eochronians could take credit for the idea like they could for other historic architectural influences.

A loud click snapped his attention back to the present.

He had a visitor. Two, to be precise.

The first was a man wearing a high-ranking military uniform and intimidating expression whom Knox assumed was Verity's father based on the familial resemblance. Knox had heard the man often while observing Verity but he'd never actually seen him. General Landau looked like he would rather come to the other side of the glass and attack him, but Knox watched him take a deep breath and square his shoulders. The move was so reminiscent of Verity, it was clear from whom she'd learned the behavior.

Another, slightly shorter man in a suit stood next to him. Even in the dim light, Knox could see there was too much product in his hair, giving him a greasy appearance. A gold emblem was attached to his hip. An obvious sign that the man was an enforcement agent of some sort.

"It's very nice to meet you. I'm Special Agent Kaur," he introduced himself, confirming Knox's deduction. "We're going to be spending a lot of time together, and I look forward to getting to know you." The words were friendly but almost aggressive.

Beside him, the general rolled his eyes.

Knox suppressed a smile. There was no reason for an inter-rogator to introduce himself to a prisoner, and doing so only armed a captive with information. Surely a special agent would know that? Or, perhaps the man was a fool.

If he was, though, Knox had to wonder why the general was suffering his presence. The agent was clearly not part of the general's group based on his title, clothes, and general air of incompetence. Verity wouldn't have stood for the idiocy, and Knox doubted she learned that behavior without any modeling from her parent.

"I hope you're in a sharing mood."

Knox watched the man pull a metallic strip out of his jacket pocket. A wrapper that revealed a neon yellowish-green rectangle that disappeared into his mouth.

Unprofessional given the setting, but it got worse. The man started chewing with his mouth open, giving Knox an unwanted, sustained view of the slimy substance. And the noise made him want to punch the agent in the throat just to shut him up.

"I understand you're responsible for kidnapping the general's daughter last month?" The words were punctuated by the squishing sound of every bite.

Knox didn't respond other than forcing himself to not let his irritation show. It was obvious everyone already knew the answer, so he doubted Verity's father was waiting for a legitimate response but he knew showing any emotion would be seized upon as a way to undermine him.

The agent's expression seemed greedy for information, though not in a true pursuit of knowledge. He seemed eager to get all he could out of Knox for personal gain, perhaps a promo-tion or recognition for successfully breaking the alien king in interrogation. A nonsensical fantasy, if there ever was one. And the agent was either delusional or so narcissistic that he believed failure to be impossible.

His tone didn't convey any concern for Verity's well-being. Knox wasn't the only one to pick up on the callousness, either, based on the muscle ticking in her father's jaw.

"You're not human nor from this planet but you've obviously had us under observation."

It wasn't a question. Not that Knox would have answered even if it was. Interrogating him was an absolute waste of everyone's time but he was curious to see how long the general would let this agent's farce go on. The statements themselves weren't wrong but repeating facts wasn't an effective way to go about it. No human was going to trick him into confirming with a wild conjecture on their part by having him fall into a habit of agreeing with his statements.

The general looked like he might have questions for Knox but was clearly holding himself back in front of the third party. Knox had to assume, then, those unspoken questions were of a more personal nature. Probably about Verity.

He could appreciate not wanting to reveal those details in front of the sleazy agent who obviously had some agenda of his own. Knox wasn't sure what it was but it struck him in a similar manner to Eiz'm and even Quallokh's self-serving nature.

"How did you find Earth?" There was barely a breath before another question came. "Was it random or targeted?"

It was so stupid he couldn't help but taunt the man. "What do you think?"

Knox tilted his head, listening to the man's heart start to beat faster in excitement, as if he really believed Knox's response was the first sign of him beginning to open up.

"How did you target people to take?"

Knox let his gaze slide over to the general. Had he not enlightened the agent? Though it was clear the agent wasn't in his employ, they were obviously working together.

What use was it to keep information from each other if you were on the same side against a common enemy?

Compartmentalizing of information only worked if there were different levels of an operation.

His soldiers, for example, didn't need to know the scientific details of his project the same way his research team didn't need to know how to interrogate humans—only how to formulate the truth serum used.

But why would the general let the agent lead the line of questioning if he didn't already have the full picture—at least from the human perspective?

Knox had to wonder if the general wanted the greaseball to fail but he couldn't think of any reason why that would be the case.

WHEN THE SPECIAL agent finally gave up on asking him questions, Knox released a sigh of relief. It was almost painful to contain his amusement at the futile exercise and the general's increasing annoyance with his companion.

Knox watched as he pulled out his phone and typed something on it. With physical keyboards, there was a unique sound to each key but it was quieter for touch-screen phones. He wondered who and what he was saying.

The general turned to the agent. "We're done for now. Someone will escort you out." His tone left no room for argument though the agent looked like he was still about to object as his mouth opened in silent outrage.

Verity's father didn't look at the man while they waited for the agent to leave. Instead, the general kept his gaze trained on Knox, as if willing him dead by the hatred in his eyes.

For all of Verity's emotions he'd seen during their time together, he'd never actually seen her hateful. Monumentally pissed-off, sure. But that was heated. The hatred he saw here was almost as cold as his own blood.

He hoped he never saw Verity look at him that way.

Once Kaur was finally gone, the general took a step closer to the glass.

"You're lucky you're not dead," he said in a deep and gravelly voice. "Because if it were solely up to me, you would already be six-feet under."

Even if he didn't understand the saying, it was clearly a death threat. But Knox knew it derived from the minimum depth to bury a body to avoid attracting wild animals.

Eochronians preferred what humans called cremation. It was the hottest they ever got, and it was only after death. If he ever got a chance to tell Verity that, he was sure she'd find some amusement in the irony.

"But luckily for you, you're more useful alive right now. The moment you outlive your usefulness, I will take great pleasure in ending you after what you did to my daughter."

He personally hadn't done much to Verity, though he certainly still wanted to do a lot to—and with—her. But he wasn't going to correct the man. It would likely only add fuel to his rage.

Knox admired the man's bravery and confidence, but it was sadly misplaced. If the general ever came at him, he'd be able to put him down very quickly. Though Verity would probably never forgive him for it, even if he refused to fight her father and merely dodged. There wouldn't be any scenario where he could win with her if her father decided to attempt to make good on his threat.

"I need to know what happened between you."

"Then you should ask her," he said. Because he wasn't about to share his side of the equation. Verity was probably already painting him as a villain and his point of view wasn't going to change the human's mind.

In issues of injustice, silence was complacency and complicity on the side of the oppressor. In instances like this, it was easily the best policy to avoid escalation.

"Don't tell me what to do," the man snapped. "You're going to sit here, alone and in the dark, until you're ready to talk."

If they literally waited that long, Knox would be almost frozen without any starlight to energize him in the basement and the general would be a pile of bones. And Verity would be, too. Her hybrid genes didn't make her a full Eochronian, so he assumed she would still have a human lifespan even after the treatment was completed.

He'd have to ask Dr. Mak'en to confirm his suspicions once he was alone again. Hopefully, he'd have better luck contacting her than he had Aerue.

Sensing he was done speaking, Verity's father narrowed his eyes and slowly retreated toward the door, refusing to turn his back on him. He had better manners than Eiz'm in that regard, though Knox was sure the general was more concerned about turning his back to an enemy than showing the proper deference to royalty.

Knox watched the man leave and let his head fall back over the edge of the chair to release the tension that had accumulated there. If every interrogation went similarly, he was in for a long stay before he could get to Verity.

He wished yet again that he'd been able to plant a listening device on her. The silence was killing him, and waiting to hear from his agents was starting to feel like a small eternity on its own.

4

VERITY

THERE WAS a knock on her door indicating the official start of another day.

Verity stretched and didn't do much else. She refused to kick off her blankets. She hadn't slept well at all, plagued by more dreams of Knox, Harrison, and Ben.

There was another knock—which meant it clearly wasn't her father.

She turned and saw the clock said eight. Which meant she'd actually slept in for the first time in forever.

Had her father come in earlier and tried to wake her up? If he had, why hadn't he persisted until she was awake? Was this another small way he was trying to apologize for his overbearing actions lately?

Her father wouldn't do that—would he?

A third knock sounded.

"Come in," she called.

McDonald opened the door and took in the fact that she was still in bed. "Why aren't you dressed? Fight training starts in ten, and we're going to be late."

"I don't want to go today," she said.

"But the general—"

"Isn't here," she countered. "And if I go today, everyone is going to blame me for Ben's death. You know they will," she added before he could lie to her and say otherwise. "I don't feel like dealing with that bullshit today."

"That's great, and understandable, but your dad might actually kill me if I mess up again, so can we please go? Besides, no one wants to be demoted like Chapman and Davies, so they'll keep their traps shut."

He was probably right, but that didn't change the fact that she wasn't going today. He and her father couldn't make her. And she'd shield him from her father's wrath if it came down to it.

"If you don't want me to miss fight training, then you can spar with me here. But I'm not leaving the house right now."

He stared at her then sighed once he realized that was her best offer.

"Fine. Just so you know, Flynn is outside now and Hughes is in the house with me today."

She nodded. She hadn't really met him but if her father had assigned him, he couldn't be bad. Unless he was another alien mole. But if she thought too much about that possibility, she wouldn't be able to function at all.

Dr. Hudson said progress wasn't linear, but she bet it would be hard for even the good psychiatrist to call this obvious setback anything else. And if she did, Verity wouldn't believe her. The F.I.N.E. acronym about repressed feelings might be hokey but at least it was true. Lying about backward being forward was outright ridiculous.

Now that she knew she didn't have to drag her butt down to the training asphalt, staying in bed longer seemed juvenile and pointless.

Verity sighed and swung her feet to the side of her bed. She stood and walked to her closet, grabbing the first top and pair of pants she encountered, too lazy to go searching for a specific outfit. She'd put her winter clothes away into drawers so there wasn't any danger of accidentally grabbing a long-sleeve top. That would be hell to do fight-training in now that she seemed to sweat as much as any other person. She missed her days when she didn't, but she now wondered if that had been a side-effect of having some alien DNA—it was the only explanation that made sense but she had no idea how to confirm it without sounding like a crazy person. If that were the case, though, why was she sweating more *now* when she probably had *more* alien DNA?

She obviously hadn't been able to ask Knox what was specifically done to her before they'd been interrupted, but she planned to ask him once she got the chance. He might not be a scientist but he was clearly the type of leader who got down to the nitty-gritty of details and she had no doubt that anything his team of experimenters knew he did, too.

Of course, as her father and Ben pointed out more than once, she had no guarantee that he would tell her the truth. But regardless of their understandable skepticism and distrust of her captor, she had the gut feeling that he'd never directly lied to her. She knew a lie of omission was still a lie, but the distinction felt monumental when it came to the alien king.

Verity grabbed her brush and winced as she entangled so many knots that it might as well have been a rat's nest. The problem with her hair was that it never looked knotty but that was a lie. It's why she always wore her hair pulled back, but even her ponytail gathered knots. She opted today for a French braid and did it while she paced her room as a pathetic warm-up before she probably had her ass handed to her by McDonald.

She remembered Zeph and Ben being shocked at her braiding without a mirror and smiled. It was such a silly thing to latch onto but with Ben now gone, she wasn't about to question or ignore any memory she had with him. Most of them were happy, anyway, so there was no reason to shove them away.

Verity ran down the stairs as she tied off her braid and saw Hughes sitting at the makeshift security station which was fast becoming a permanent fixture now that another cyber dog had visited the previous day to connect the cameras from Knox's cell to their monitors.

She hadn't been able to bring herself to check out her father's interrogation with Knox yet, but she'd probably do it after fight training.

McDonald was waiting for her in the living room and had already moved the coffee table and her dance barre out of the way to give them as much floor space as possible.

He rolled his neck setting off a series of pops that sounded louder than usual now that her hearing had gotten an alien-boost. Almost as if they were her own joints popping in her ears.

"Ready?" he asked.

As she ever would be. Verity had beaten McDonald in the past but only once, and that was when she was confident in having full control of her body.

The dizziness wasn't any less severe, but it was thankfully less frequent. She'd stopped doing arabesques so that could also be a contributing factor.

The nausea was also less prevalent, but there was a near-constant stomach ache in her muscles from all her bouts of vomiting. It temporarily got worse with every episode.

He stepped forward. She easily side-stepped his grasp but failed to notice his foot hooking her ankle until she was already going down.

He offered his hand to pull her up.

Verity accepted and jumped to her feet, then swayed a little. Bad idea.

"That was pathetic," he said.

She nodded in agreement. She put her hands up and steadied her stance. "Again."

He laid her out again even though she avoided the same trick.

She glared up at him.

"You asked for it."

"Don't be a smart-ass." She pushed herself up to sitting and then stood up slower than last time. "You knew I wasn't being literal."

"I didn't want to assume because it would make an ass out of u and me."

"You still assumed I was literally asking to be beaten again which means the only ass here is you." She surged forward, grabbed his shoulder and blocked his other arm from hitting her head, but then he grabbed her hair and yanked.

She refused to let go and kicked his kneecap in retaliation.

He bent his legs and flipped her over his back before she could kick the other one and force him to his knees.

He chuckled.

"See, you really did need fight training today. Aren't you glad you didn't skip it?"

"I'm sure my muscles would be happier if I had."

She was already getting a bit sore from hitting the carpet three times already. But he was right. She needed to stay at the top of her self-defense game and get used to fighting when she wasn't at peak physical health. She still had no idea how to resolve her symptoms since her return.

If she fought them now, they'd probably be able to grab her from under her father and guards' noses without a problem.

Verity rolled to her side and pushed herself to her feet again.

She stared at her opponent, trying to find a weak spot.

And then it happened.

A red glow appeared around him. Not like a superhero flame or red smoke, or even like what a mystical aura was said to look like.

It was like he was *emanating* the red heat and it moved with him.

Seeing her freeze, McDonald must have realized something wrong because he left his fighting stance and instead gently rested a hand on her shoulder and led her to sit on the couch.

"Are you okay?"

She shook her head.

"Should I call your dad?"

"No. But maybe you could get me some water?"

Instead, he called out, "Hughes! Glass of water for Verity."

She heard the other guard walk into the kitchen and open the cabinet. Then water was running.

She zeroed in on the sound while she stared at one spot on the floor. There wasn't any red in her vision looking at it, but when she looked at McDonald, it was still there.

Was it him? Had she been duped yet again in believing a friend was human?

Hughes came in and handed her the water before leaving without a word and returning to the security room.

He moved fast, but she saw the red outline around him and fainter traces of red in the space he'd just vacated.

Verity squeezed her eyes shut and groaned. What the hell was happening to her?

She was sick of not knowing the answers to an ever-growing list of questions.

There had to be a solution, but the only ones who could give them to her were also the ones responsible for her predicament in the first place.

She didn't need to talk about it to Dr. Hudson to know that it was a dire situation of dependency.

She hadn't been able to sever the strange connection she had with Knox, and now she couldn't until she found out how to survive without him.

A devious trick if she'd ever thought of one. Even worse than drug companies who advertised to addiction-prone people.

Knox didn't strike her as an evil mastermind, but his plan was still one that would make any villain proud.

She just had to hope her story was more of a fairytale where the hero triumphed against all odds. Otherwise, she'd be in deep trouble.

5

KNOX

KNOX TURNED his gaze back to the door.

He had more visitors.

And he recognized both sets of footsteps.

A moment passed before the general appeared. A female doctor accompanied the surly man.

She stepped forward until she was almost in front of the glass before the general grabbed her forearm, preventing her from going any closer.

Knox couldn't help but smile.

The man was right to be fearful but he'd never hurt a woman. And particularly not this one. She was one of his, after all.

"My daughter said she was experimented on during her imprisonment," the general said. "We'll see how much you like it."

"Oh?" he asked.

"My name is Dr. Lane," his mole said, introducing herself to him as if they truly were strangers. "We'll be spending a lot of time together."

Wonderful. Perhaps she had answers that Zeph hadn't been able to acquire.

"How tall are you?"

"Why don't you measure me yourself?"

She smiled serenely at him. "I'm not stupid, so please refrain from attempting to trick me. It won't work."

He smiled. He was sure the general assumed he was amused by the doctor, which was true—her act as a human was very entertaining—but he was actually reacting to the collaborative trick they were pulling off on him.

"How much would you estimate?"

"I don't have your human measurement systems memorized," he lied. "And if you're as intelligent as you would like me to believe, I'm sure you can come up with an accurate value."

She pulled out a smartphone and noted something in the device.

"Are you average for your species?"

"Certainly not," he said, putting as much offense into his tone as possible. His royal blood and persuasion powers removed that possibility but if she had asked about specific things—like height and build—his answer could vary a little. He wasn't too proud to deny he was not the best in everything. He wasn't nearly as scientifically intelligent as either Dr. Makzik and her sister Dr. Mak'en, which was why he had delegated them to handle his project on Earth and on his ship. When he'd put it to the genius twins which would go undercover on Earth, Dr. Makzik had come forward and adopted the persona of Dr. Lane, quickly proving her brilliance to undergraduate and medical education institutions that allowed her to gain authentic human credentials after another mole had impeccably falsified her elementary and high school transcripts.

At the time, Knox had no idea that she would become Verity's doctor but the timing had been perfect. By the time the fictional Dr. Lane had applied for the job of doctor at Groom Lake, she was obviously overqualified and was hired immediately.

"Does your kind procreate sexually or asexually?" she asked him in a detached voice, as if she didn't already know the answer.

Knox could see Verity's father visibly start at the question. He probably didn't want to know the answer if it affected his daughter's stay in space, but Knox chose not to lie. There was no reason to.

"Sexually," he answered. "We're not that different from humans that way."

The general glared at him but didn't interrupt.

"How else do you resemble humanity?"

"You're going to have to be more specific."

"Do you have two hearts?"

He shook his head. Zeph had once mentioned a popular TV show where aliens had two of the life-giving organ so he supposed it wasn't the most outlandish question to ask.

"What is your expected lifespan?"

"Very long compared to short human years," he said.

"How old are you?"

"Already incredibly old by Earth's standards," he said. It was a silly thing but he didn't want Verity learning his age from anyone other than directly from him. He'd already side-stepped her question during one of their shared meals but now that she knew Trohm's true age, he was certain she was already thinking differently of him.

It might be naïve of him to still wish for it, but he wanted to maintain as equal a footing between them—if she knew how superior Eochronians were to humans, she'd never trust him. And he wanted her to like him as much as he did her.

Dr. Makzik turned to the general. "May I?" she asked.

He opened the door through which they entered and they left. Knox could hear their footsteps through the wall until he heard the door behind him unlock.

His mole walked up to his side and he saw a needle in her hand. With his hand blocked from the human's perspective, he removed his armor from the arm so she could draw some of his blood.

There was no way she'd actually reveal their genetic secrets to humanity, and he didn't want the general to realize there was an invisible barrier protecting him from the outside world. Otherwise, he'd be quizzed about Eochronian technology and he didn't feel like handling them if it was avoidable.

He schooled his feature against the unpleasant sting of the metal piercing his arm. It was much thicker than any technology used by them. The needles used to administer their truth serum were intentionally more painful which was why Eiz'm loved utilizing the method even when it was unnecessary. Thankfully, his engineers were able to produce it quickly in vast quantities or they would be in danger of inconveniently running out.

For medical tests, they often used the adhesive method Verity had been subjected to against his orders. Humans had recently invented something closer but they were still very far behind in finding a painless method.

He watched his iridescent blue blood fill the chamber. Regardless of what lies Dr. Makzik told the humans, he had to assume the general saw that his blood was visibly different from theirs. He knew human blood was blue inside until it was oxidized, turning it red.

Perhaps his mole would be able to sell the idea that Eochronians didn't need oxygen to survive. It was partially true, but they were like the largest mammal on Earth—they could go without it for longer than a human but they still needed it. Now that he considered it, such a lie could potentially backfire if the general decided to cut the oxygen in his cell. She would surely come up with something without problematic consequences.

A thought occurred to him that made him waver. Was there a chance that she had switched allegiances in her long stay on Earth? He hadn't been in contact with her as regularly as his other moles. He had been periodically updated on the genetic progress of the general's misguided experiment as the human's tinkering was the basis of his own project, but there was a lot of leeway for her to have secretly turned against him.

While the needle was still in him, he watched Dr. Makzik attach another vial. Only after that was filled, did she remove the contraption. Knox cursed as the needle was pulled out. He had felt it in his arm the whole time but its movement briefly exacerbated the uncomfortable sensation. With one hand, she placed the needle and connected contraption in her jacket pocket, and shook the vials with her free hand.

Not only were humans inefficient in drawing blood, apparently they were also wasteful in their testing. Eochronian technology could take a quarter of the amount for the same number of experiments. They were much better at maximizing the sample than humanity.

He knew she was probably thinking the same thing.

As if responding to his thoughts, she met his gaze and gave him a quick wink, causing his anxiety to dissipate. They were still on the same team.

He couldn't contain the curse that dropped from his mouth when she applied an antiseptic to the open wound. He would heal in a few moments but not even Eochronian healing was that fast. Her application of an adhesive bandage only irritated the area more, as he could feel the stickiness more than he expected humans could. Why else would they tolerate such uncomfortable material as medical after-care?

"Are you done?" the general demanded behind him.

If the man had hoped to startle Knox, he had been unsuccessful, but he had to admire the intimidation effort.

"Yes, sir," Dr. Makzik answered, stepping out of the compartment.

Knox waited to hear them both leave but the general didn't move away. Instead, the man's footsteps got louder as they neared a second before Knox saw the fist coming at him.

Instead of dodging, he let the hit land.

"That was for my daughter," he growled. Another hit was aimed at his other cheek. "And that was for Tenner."

Then the human let loose a slew of punches in quick succession, forgoing an explanation for every attack.

The blows didn't hurt, but Knox pretended to be in pain by wincing and moving his jaw in an exaggerated manner.

"I'm sorry for your loss, but I was not responsible for his demise."

He had to wonder if Verity had passed along the message already or if her father didn't believe Knox was innocence. He wasn't certain even *she* believed him but if any human would, it would be her.

"Excuse me if I don't take your word for it," the man sneered.

Knox didn't answer. He knew that his witty responses always annoyed Verity but also amused her at some level, even if she wouldn't admit it out loud. He was certain her father would not react the same way and Knox had no desire to earn another blow from the general.

At some point, even he would feel the compounded effect of multiple attacks. But what concerned him more was the increased likelihood that the man would break his hand and then Verity would blame him for her father's injury—despite his passive role in the exchange. He was merely sitting in a chair, after all, while her father loomed over him with the apparent upper hand.

"How many more moles do you have here?"

The man was intelligent but Knox wasn't going to make it easy on him. He stayed silent.

"One?"

If they were only talking about this military base at this moment, yes. If he meant the planet, the number was much higher.

"How long have your kind been here?"

He'd throw him a crumb. "A long time." Trohm's stint as the

human Tristan was twenty-four years, which was already a decent amount of time for an undercover mission by human standards. If he told the general about the millions of years they'd been secretly living among humanity, his poor mind would likely explode.

The man leaned down, bringing their faces closer. "I don't know what you did to my daughter while you had her, but rest assured, you will *never* get close to her again."

Knox kept his expression blank and refused to break eye contact with the general. A good leader knew which battles to avoid, but as Knox and the human were not on equal footing, he refused to act *excessively* weak. It was effective to let him believe he had been subdued by the chains but there was nothing to gain from pretending to cower.

If Verity's father were an Eochronian, Knox might have looked away to avoid escalating the situation because he was sure the man would be at least as skilled as Dhaca and perhaps even Aerue. Now that he thought about it, his curiosity was piqued but he knew he'd likely never get an answer as the general hadn't signed himself up for his own genetic experiment program like he had his daughter.

Knox couldn't be upset that Verity was involved, even if it was against her will and knowledge, as it led him to meeting her. But he did think it rather unfair that the general played god with his daughter's life in a matter he wasn't willing to experience first-hand. If things had gone terribly wrong, Knox wondered if the man would have felt guilt or if he would have found some way to absolve himself of blame.

Feeling a burst of anger on Verity's behalf, Knox spoke. "I think that's up for your daughter to decide."

He was met with a punch to his nose, and he could feel a small trickle of blood move down to his upper lip.

Impressive. Anger clearly made the man stronger. A motivator rather than a paralytic agent. He'd have to remember that.

"She'll do as she's told," the man said.

Knox sincerely doubted that. He heard the man leave and the door locking behind him.

His eyes found one of the cameras and he smiled up at the lens. Something told him she'd see it, and when she did, she wouldn't be able to resist his silent challenge.

He couldn't wait to see her again.

6

VERITY

VERITY SAT in the exam room and waited for Dr. Lane.

She'd texted her father's assistant to make an appointment for her and had been told that her doctor was busy.

Which meant that something big had to be happening because her father had definitely made her needs a priority for the woman.

Verity had a feeling that she was probably with her father interrogating Knox but she still wasn't yet ready to watch the security footage in real-time. She had watched Special Agent Kaur question Knox and even though the camera angle wasn't super close to the alien king, she could still tell that he was amused by the annoying man.

Her father's stiff body language also told her that he still wanted to punch the man over his disrespect for her during their last meeting together.

Verity thanked her lucky stars that he hadn't asked for a follow-up session. Now that he was also questioning Knox, though, she had a feeling her good luck on that front was going to run out soon.

Her father had been gone for over three hours already, and she had no idea how much longer he'd be occupied.

She wasn't exactly *hiding* her visit to Dr. Lane—she had called her father's assistant after all—but she didn't want to answer his questions about why until she had a better answer than "I don't know."

Even though he'd kept the huge secret of her true nature from her, she still felt obliged to tell him about her health. At least, her physical health. She was enjoying not having to tell him about her therapy. Aside from her liaison with Tristan, she had never needed to keep a secret from him so she'd never thought about how it was a little strange that she *always* told him everything. Even when she didn't need to share something, she felt compelled to anyway. Verity didn't have things to hide but she realized had no expectation of privacy between her and her dad. It was just another aspect of individuation she hadn't ever experienced, according to Dr. Hudson.

She wished she could create the same boundary in this situation, but her life-long habit of him always knowing was hard to break.

Verity lay down on the exam table and closed her eyes.

Some time later, she woke up to the door opening.

She sat up and saw Dr. Lane walk in.

"Sorry for the long wait, Verity," the woman apologized. "What can I do for you today?"

Verity looked at the woman and was surprised to see no red around her. She'd seen it around everyone she, McDonald, and Hughes had passed on her way to the appointment.

She rubbed her eyes just to make sure but nothing appeared.

Maybe she was already better?

"Are you okay, Verity?"

"I've been seeing weird things."

"Can you be more descriptive? Are things distorted? Black spots? Fuzzy?"

"I'm seeing red outlines of people."

Dr. Lane removed the light scope from where it hung on the wall and removed the cap that normally went into someone's ear.

"I want you to follow the light," she instructed, before turning it on.

Verity resisted the urge to blink and did as she was told.

Dr. Lane stepped closer until she was right in front of her and held one eyelid up and then the other.

Finally, the light switched off.

Verity blinked and could feel tears gathering in her eyes to rehydrate them.

"Well?" she asked.

"I don't see anything that would physically cause your altered vision but we can do an eye test if you'd like to. Otherwise, perhaps take a break from looking at screens. Doing so without enough breaks can cause eye fatigue. You could also try blue-light blocking glasses which help diminish headaches caused by eye-strain."

That all sounded fine but she'd definitely stared at screens for long period of times throughout her life without ever having red invade her vision. And the timing of this symptom along with everything else was too big a coincidence to ignore.

"What if that doesn't solve it?"

"Then we can consult an ophthalmologist."

Luckily there was one in the building because going off base to a civilian one would be a pain. Finding one who took insurance was paramount, and she had no idea how many options that would leave. After all, medical bills were no joke.

And while she benefitted from a great medical plan as the daughter of a general on base, she knew everyone else wasn't as lucky.

"How long should I wait to contact you again?"

"Let's give it a week. How does that sound?"

"Will any blue-light blocking pair of glasses work?"

Dr. Lane nodded.

Thank goodness for one-day shipping.

"Are there any other symptoms you're experiencing?"

"I'm still feeling dizzy every so often."

"Has it gotten better?"

She shrugged. Frequency wasn't the only way to measure a symptom.

"What about the nausea and vomiting?"

"Still there," Verity answered.

She watched Dr. Lane make a note on her clipboard.

"I'm going to give you a prescription that I think will help with both. It might also affect your inner-ear so if you experience some minor equilibrium problems, don't be alarmed. But if you find yourself experiencing it to a troublesome degree, let me know and I can lower the dosage."

Verity nodded. How much did it suck that medicine meant to alleviate one set of symptoms also came with its own unpleasant collection?

"If you don't have any other concerns to discuss with me, I'll go get you the medicine."

Verity nodded and waited, swinging her legs just to do something while she waited.

She wasn't alone for long before Dr. Lane returned and handed her a pill bottle. "This is a sample that should be enough to get you through the week while the prescription is shipped here."

Verity read the label but didn't recognize the name of the drug, though it sounded like some that she'd taken in the past. Probably in the same family. Honestly, she didn't really care what it was as long as it helped her.

The written instructions said "Take as needed."

"Is that when I think I'm going to vomit or…?" She trailed off as she considered her words. Certainly doing it then would merely waste the medicine by bringing it back up with the rest of her stomach's contents.

"Take it no more than twice a day, and if you feel like you're starting to feel unwell but not imminently in danger of having an episode. Otherwise, wait until afterward. I also recommend taking it with some light food in your stomach," Dr. Lane explained. "If you have any more questions, you can call the office and leave a message for me."

Verity jumped to her feet. "Thank you," she said. "I know this was short notice."

"Of course, Verity. I hope you feel better soon."

Verity walked out into the waiting room and found McDonald and Hughes pacing. They were surrounded by red but the whole room seemed to be filled with the color now in horizontal streaks tracing their walking paths like a long-exposure photograph.

Hughes stopped first.

"You done?" McDonald asked.

She nodded.

Verity waved goodbye to the receptionist as she walked past to the elevators.

"You okay?" McDonald asked her as they watched the numbers light up, indicating their descent to the ground floor.

"I will be," she answered. And for the first time in a while, she truly believed it.

7

KNOX

DR. MAKZIK WAS BACK. This time, the general wasn't with her, which allowed them to speak freely as long as they kept it at a sub-audible frequency.

He'd been worried Verity's eagle-eyed father would notice his mouth moving without accompanying sound if he'd tried to secretly communicate with his mole right in front of him. There was no reason to encourage more suspicion on the human's side.

"Here to draw more blood?" he asked at a normal volume.

"Not today," the doctor replied, smiling at him.

"Then what?"

"Well, I wanted to test your reflexes, but it's pointless with you tied up like this."

"Did you ask them to release me for your scientific investigation?"

She gave him a stern look, and he suppressed a laugh. He watched her move between him and the camera, her back blocking both her and him from the lens, allowing them to speak freely without fear of their lips being read.

"What did you do with my blood?" he asked, now speaking too softly for humans to hear.

"I ran a Chem 7, CBC, and a Blood Arterial Gas test."

"Translation?" He was generally pretty on top of human vernacular but he hadn't seen the need to deep dive into their medical jargon. Perhaps it had been a mistake, but at the very least, he had Dr. Makzik who could explain things to him.

"Chemical breakdown, blood count, and oxygen levels." Her answer was unhesitant, coming almost automatically.

He was impressed with how deep she'd gotten into her role on Earth.

"They're standard tests and I would be expected to run them on you," she continued. "They will show anomalies which I can truthfully report without my having to explain the actual differences between us and humans. You'd be surprised how much time can be bought with the simple phrase, 'I need to conduct more research.'"

He could say the same for Eochronians, though he supposed he was more interfering with Dr. Mak'en's work than the general seemed to be with Dr. Makzik. Which was good for their purposes. "Doesn't human impatience get in the way?"

"Sometimes" she murmured.

"What are you supposedly doing today?"

"Taking measurements." She removed a ribbon with lines at evenly-spaced intervals.

He held still as she measured the circumference of his head. Before he could ask what the point was, she spoke.

"She came to see me."

He didn't need clarification on who they were now talking about.

"How is she?"

"Not doing well, Your Majesty. She's still experiencing dizziness and nausea, but she recently started seeing infrared."

"Does she know that's what it is?"

"I don't believe so, but she's very intelligent. I wouldn't be surprised if she put it together by the end of today."

"What did you do?"

"I gave her some treatment pills. They should help with her transition."

"So, you believe her symptoms are her human side fighting her new Eochronian DNA?"

"Yes," Dr. Makzik answered. "When I did her blood test following her return, I recognized more of our genetic markers in her. She and her father have no idea the specifics, but I did have to tell him something. I've been in on the secret of her genetically engineered status since the beginning," she added at his questioning look. "If I don't say anything is out of the ordinary, it'll make him suspicious."

Knox nodded. It made sense, but he didn't like the idea of Dr. Makzik having to reveal anything true about their kind, especially to a man smart enough to weaponize that information to the greatest effect within his human limitations.

The general wasn't a politician who sometimes put aside logic for more self-serving and power-hungry goals. No, the man would take all he learned and use it immediately, without wasting any time on implementing new and effective systems for the betterment of humanity. Again, Knox had to admit he admired Verity's father. His actions were strict but his heart was in the right place, and he didn't let ego get in the way of accomplishing his objectives.

Unfortunately, their goals were in opposition.

Dr. Makzik had moved on to measuring his arms and he knew that she was mentally keeping track of the numbers.

"What will you do when she starts having more symptoms?" He had no idea what they would be, as she was the only subject who was transforming quickly, but he was almost certain there would be more. She could potentially even experience a growth spurt to better match Eochronians but he couldn't count on that. He was curious how else she would change.

"What percentage is she at?" he asked.

"Seventy-three."

Almost another ten percent increase since the last update he'd received when she was still on the ship. Twenty percent in less than a month? Her progress was miraculous and better than he ever could have hoped for.

And now it made even more sense for her body to be having a hard time with such a rapid pace of change.

"Do you think she's reached her maximum?" he asked.

Dr. Mak'en had believed there would be a cap at around seventy-five even after a full and successful treatment, but a part of him hoped Verity would prove that hypothesis wrong.

If they could create pure Eochronians from humans, then his detractors wouldn't be able to use that as a point of contention anymore, and it would be easier to pull them back to his side and away from Eiz'm.

Which reminded him, he needed to contact Aerue again.

"Have you heard from your sister?" he asked Dr. Makzik.

She shook her head. "I'll try to contact her, Your Majesty. Is something wrong?"

"Just make sure she's alright," he said.

She nodded and finally finished her ministrations. She stepped back and bowed her head ever so slightly as she moved around him and left the room.

He doubted the humans watching the security footage would notice it, but she hadn't turned her back on him the whole time, and it just was another reminder of Eiz'm's insubordination.

He waited until Dr. Makzik was out of hearing range before he opened a communication link to Aerue. Again, he was left waiting for an answer before it shut down, having failed to make the connection.

Knox was about to try again when he saw Trohm contacting him.

"Yes?" he answered.

Knox watched Trohm look quickly to his left and right before quietly saying, "You were right, Your Majesty."

"About what, specifically?"

"Eiz'm is using the Vruxols as his personal army to back him up."

It was just as he feared.

"Are there any still loyal to me?"

"Aside from me and Zeph?"

Knox gave him a look that he hoped conveyed his impatience for him to get to the point.

"Dr. Mak'en and her team, and Aerue. I hear Aerue is being locked up in the dungeons."

"Why aren't you?"

Trohm shook his head. "I'm not really sure."

Knox wasn't sure whether to believe him. He'd avoided Arfilmea's attempt at a similar manipulation. But as he wasn't planning on returning anytime soon, even if Trohm had secretly switched sides, his talking to him wouldn't lead to an effective trap.

"Let me know of any other important developments," he said before ending the call.

He leaned back against the cold metal headrest and considered his options. If he showed up immediately, Eiz'm would probably be waiting for him. Because even if Trohm hadn't betrayed him, the only reason Knox could think of his enemy leaving the agent alone was if he was using him as unsuspecting bait.

At the same time, if he waited too long, he might not have any supporters left by the time he returned. And now that Verity had unknowingly resumed her treatment, it was a ripe opportunity to spirit her away back to his ship. On the other hand, if Dr. Mak'en and her team were imprisoned, they wouldn't be able to safely oversee Verity's progress like Dr. Makzik could. Which meant his best course of action was to wait a little longer.

But he was getting bored, and that only led to impulsive decisions. And he couldn't afford to start making mistakes now. Not after everything he'd already done to get to this point.

8

VERITY

AFTER GETTING the all-clear from Hughes that her room was safe, Verity ran upstairs and took a pill.

She knew Dr. Lane had said as needed but she wanted to be sure she wasn't going to embarrass herself during another fight session. After interrupting the last one, she had asked McDonald to humor her with another go at it later.

She realized she'd forgotten to ask Dr. Lane how long the medicine took to go into effect but she had a feeling it wouldn't be instant.

"I'm going to watch the recordings first," she called out to McDonald as she walked into the security room.

Hughes was already seated at the set up so she grabbed a set of headphones and plugged them into the monitor on the other side of the room. She didn't want to interrupt his ability to keep tabs on current activity around the home. That was his main job, after all, now that Knox was currently tied up.

She moved the mouse to wake up the screen and clicked on the most recently created file. The footage started playing in front of her and she found herself wishing yet again that it had a closer shot of Knox. Her improving eyesight could only help so much. Even hidden cameras could zoom, couldn't they?

She heard the footsteps before her father and Dr. Lane appeared close enough to the glass for the camera to pick up. If she had wanted to, she could watch the other angle that was on the entrance to the basement level but she really only cared about watching Knox's expressions as she listened to the conversations so reminiscent of the ones she'd been forced to have in space with Eiz'm, Aerue, and even Knox himself.

Verity felt her mood instantly dip at the comparison between them. She shouldn't be thinking about how they were similar. He was the reason she'd been kidnapped in the first place. What did she care if he was now getting some karmic justice by having the tables flipped on him?

The rational part of her knew she should probably tell Dr. Hudson about her conflicted feelings but she didn't want to be labeled with Stockholm syndrome. She shifted in her seat and looked over her shoulder to make sure Hughes didn't notice her discomfort. He was busy looking at the screens in front of him. She doubted anything would break his concentration unless he saw something on the cameras or if he heard an intruder in the house.

She took a deep breath and turned back to watching.

She blushed when Dr. Lane asked how the aliens reproduced and Knox replied, "sexually." His answer brought back the memory of her catching him with Arfilmea *in flagrant delicto*, and she really wished there was a way to permanently erase that image from her mind.

Dr. Lane was now drawing blood from Knox and even she could see it was darker than human blood. And definitely not red. It wasn't iridescent like his sweat but it appeared to be a dark, midnight blue with some hints of green, though it was hard to tell from so far away.

Dr. Lane eventually left and now her father was punching the shit out of Knox. Or, he would be if Knox were a human. She flexed her hand, remembering how hard his face was when she'd slapped him.

"You will *never* get close to her again," her father growled so low that she felt it practically vibrating her bones.

She doubted her father was doing much damage but for some reason, Knox was behaving like he had. It was obvious to her that it was an act but she couldn't figure out why he was doing it. She supposed it had to do with the same motivation that was keeping him in the chair instead of breaking out as easily as Trohm had.

She had no illusions that Trohm had stayed as long as he had because he was following Knox's orders to probably eavesdrop. But she had a feeling that Knox had been about to grab her and take her on another interstellar trip before her father's STFs had interrupted—saving her from falling victim to the same kidnapping twice.

If he was waiting to get her alone so he could whisk her away again, it would make sense why he was still in his cell. But why didn't he merely break out, overpower her guards, and take her? She knew he was easily capable of breaking free. He had insisted on his innocence regarding Harrison and Ben's deaths but she was certain he was responsible for knocking out all the guards around Trohm and breaking out his double-agent.

The hairs on the back of her neck rose and she slammed the space bar to pause the video. Verity didn't want to miss anything. She turned in her chair to check on Hughes again, who was still staring at his screen. He was impersonating a statue, sitting so stiffly she thought he might shatter if she poked him.

Verity spun back around and hit play. Now they were talking about whether she had a choice in if and when she'd be seeing Knox again. Her father insisted that she'd follow orders and while she hated to agree with the alien king, she bristled at her father's assumption that she'd fall in line like one of the men under his command.

She was his daughter for fuck's sake. Not a soldier. Never had been, never would be. And as soon as this alien business was concluded, she was going to move off base no matter what her father said.

VERITY SAT at the kitchen table slowly sipping the ice-cold water she'd left in the refrigerator overnight.

McDonald sat opposite her and was watching something on his phone. She assumed it was something related to her detail based on how intently he was staring at the screen.

She cleared her throat and he looked up.

"Ready when you are."

He nodded and stored his phone in his pocket. When they reentered the living room, he put it on the couch and took up a fighting stance. She did the same.

The red outline had disappeared, and she was so relieved she almost told McDonald about it now she was feeling better. But she kept her mouth shut. She didn't want to freak him out unnecessarily. If it became a problem again, she'd bring it up. For now, though, she narrowed her eyes and zoned in on McDonald's hands and feet, waiting for any sign that he was about to pounce.

He made his move and she dodged to the left, almost avoiding him, but he grabbed her thigh and wrapped his arm around her other knee as he pulled her down to the ground.

She barely felt the impact, frozen in her mind and body at the intimate touch.

Realistically, she knew the intent was purely platonic and for fighting efficiency but the terror running through her didn't care. Her breath was choppy, and every inhale hurt like hell, pushing against the tight band of anxiety around her chest. Her muscles seized up, trapping her in the moment, and her mind went blank.

He saw her panic because he jumped up and pulled her up by her arm. "Verity, I am so sorry! I didn't mean—I wasn't—"

He raked his fingers through his hair, looking so flustered she felt bad for him and wished she could reassure him but she still couldn't form words.

"Are you okay?" he asked, watching her warily, his eyes filled with concern.

No. She mentally shook herself. "Don't worry about me," she said. "I'm just going to take a shower."

He nodded solemnly and followed her up the stairs, keeping his distance without being asked.

She appreciated it.

Verity closed the door and started the shower. She stripped and stepped under the water. Letting the hot stream pound her back, she cursed herself for relapsing. She was sure Dr. Hudson would say she was being too tough on herself and that not all upsetting moments were genuine steps backward.

But she wasn't going to text Dr. Hudson about the incident. She didn't want to develop a habit of dependency on constantly contacting her therapist whenever something went wrong.

How else would she become an independently functional person in society if she didn't stick certain things out by herself?

She scrubbed her skin hard, not to necessarily erase McDonald's touch—she meant it when she said she didn't blame him for anything—but more to remove any body memories of what had happened to her. Verity knew it was impossible, but that didn't stop her from trying.

VERITY SHOT UP IN BED.

Her hand flew up to her forehead and came away sticky with sweat.

Now that she was awake, she felt the sheet around her legs also wet.

She threw them off and looked around her room, checking to make sure she was alone.

She didn't see any ripples in the air or strange shimmering like she'd seen the night that she'd been abducted, or even the night she and Ben had tested out whether they had any romantic and sexual chemistry on top of their friendship.

But a red light emanating upward from her phone was piercing the darkness. She walked up to her desk and grabbed her device. Was it being hacked? Or was this another instance of seeing red as she had earlier in the day?

An iridescent sheen caught the corner of her eye.

She walked closer to the full-length mirror hanging on her wall and to her surprise, found the source to be her own skin.

It almost looked like Knox's skin.

She touched her skin to double-check that she was awake instead of having a lucid dream on top of the nightmare that had woken her up in the first place.

She'd been back in the water tank on the spaceship, waiting for death to take her. But instead of the almost peaceful feeling she'd accomplished then, in her dream she was panicking and attempting to take deep breaths of air even though she was already fully submerged without any chance of not flooding her lungs with water. She was drowning from the inside out, too. And it had *hurt*. Burning her lungs and throat to the point that she thought she was being tortured by fire instead of water. Right when she thought she was about to die, she'd woken up.

Nothing changed. She pinched herself just to make sure but got the same result. Which meant she was wide awake and this was real.

Shit.

Was it too soon for another visit to Dr. Lane? She didn't exactly want to start having daily appointments for the same reason she didn't want to always be texting Dr. Hudson.

She'd just ride it out. And if she felt better with the medicine, then she wouldn't mention it. But if she kept having shiny rainbow skin, she'd have to tell Dr. Lane before her father noticed it and brought her to the doctor himself.

She changed into an even lighter pair of sleeping clothes and crawled back into bed but left the blankets off. Closing her eyes, she prayed for sleep to come quickly and for the very slim chance that she woke and this whole episode would turn out to be a bad dream.

9

KNOX

VERITY WAS FINALLY HERE to see him.

She was wearing another thin tank top and soft, billowing pajama pants that clung to her curves.

It reminded him of how he'd first met her. From what he'd observed of her, it seemed her wardrobe lacked any fancy garments, though as a general's daughter, he assumed she had to have something to wear for special events. But he enjoyed seeing her wear things he'd chosen for her and he hoped there would be another chance for that soon once he solved the Eiz'm problem.

She wasn't escorted which made him wonder how she'd gotten past her guards. Did she have to fight them like she'd fought his? Or had she been able to talk her way out of being supervised against her father's wishes?

Though Verity seemed to respect authority, it seemed her time on his ship had awakened a rebellious streak in her. Or, perhaps, she just didn't want people dictating her actions anymore. He doubted the general would appreciate a similarity between him and Knox but anyone being logical would admit that they had both controlled Verity's life in ways he was sure she would consider overbearing.

She moved closer to the glass, her feet barely making any sound as she slowly walked toward him. He could see her leg muscles tensing as she exerted control to keep her steps quiet.

He leaned forward when she finally reached the glass, straining against the chains. He didn't want to break through them just yet. Doing so would show his hand too early, though he had no doubt that she already knew that he was only staying because he wanted to.

He wanted to know how brave she was now they were back on her home planet, her "home turf" as humans liked to call it.

She walked up to the glass and touched it. Something no one else had done—not even Dr. Makzik in her human act.

He tilted his head, watching her intensely curious expression. "You're not afraid?" he asked.

"Why would I be?"

"What's to stop me from grabbing you right now?"

He expected her to step back but she didn't seem intimidated at all. Determination shone in her eyes, and he was glad to see the fire there.

But she did turn her head and started walking away.

He sat up, curious as to what her plan was. Then he heard her walking through the passageway and the door behind him opening.

Knox craned his head over his shoulder and saw Verity come into view. She walked in front of him, her back to the glass.

He expected her to press her back against the barrier for protection space would give her but instead, she walked right up to him, placing her hands on top of his and bringing her mouth within kissing distance.

"What did you do to me?" she whispered.

"What do you think?"

"You're changing me."

He could say the same, though not in an identical manner.

"Why?"

Knox felt the sudden urge to come clean. "Because I want you," he confessed.

She tilted her head, no doubt scanning his face for a sign he was being dishonest.

"I don't understand."

"That's okay," he said.

"It's not fair that you know and I don't."

"I'm sorry."

"Then tell me."

Instead, he tilted his chin as far up as his chains would allow and kissed her.

The action seemed to cut some sort of tether in her because she was leaning into him, her hands cradling his face.

And then she shocked him by sitting on his lap, straddling him and grinding on him as their tongues fought for dominance in their heated kiss.

He groaned and let himself get caught up in the passion they shared in this stolen pocket of time before he'd break free and take her with him. He was sure doing so would make her dislike him again, so for now, he would revel in what she was willingly giving him.

She pulled back for a moment but lightly bit his lip as she did, tugging on it until she let go, an impish smile gracing her beautiful face.

"I've been wanting to do that since we kissed the first time," she said, resting her forehead against his.

"Me, too."

"Then why didn't you?" She kissed him again briefly. "You had me at your mercy," she said against his lips. "Why not seduce me after dinner? Or instead of dinner?"

"I don't understand."

"It's a human thing," she said. "And at this point, I don't care. I have you now, and I'm not letting you go."

"Neither will I."

She chuckled. "You're a little tied up right now. I'm sure this is new for you."

He remembered yet again how she'd reacted to his admission that he had tied up some of his lovers.

"Next time, maybe we'll switch."

"Mmm... I don't know. I like being able to touch you." To emphasize her words, she lifted herself up enough to fit her hand between them and rubbed his growing arousal.

She then began moving her hips forwards and back, riding him through his armor and her clothes.

He flexed his hands in their restraints, holding back the urge to break them and hold her by her hair and her hip to guide her motions. She was moving painfully slow and he would make sure to speed her up.

But he decided to thrust his hips up when she did her next downstroke, earning a moan from her, and her head tilting back.

Luckily, she was still close enough for him to latch his lips around the sensitive spot between her neck and shoulder. He began kissing and sucking it, which seemed to drive her crazy as another moan dropped from her mouth and her hands tightened in his hair, holding him in place.

Then she rotated her head so she could also reach his neck and sunk her teeth into his shoulder, letting out a scream into his flesh as she fell apart in his lap, her orgasm making her tremble above him.

He jolted beneath her and continued thrusting until he found his own release.

Knox jerked forward in the chair, blinking rapidly and scanning his surroundings in the dark.

No remaining heat signatures of any visitors. He was totally alone.

When was the last time he'd experienced such a vivid dream? On his ship, also about Verity, if his memory served. But even that hadn't felt as real as this had.

He looked down and saw his arousal was still going strong, his dream release being nothing more than a figment of his imagination. He took a few deep breaths, willing the tension to abate, but it didn't help.

He grit his teeth and glanced at the cameras, hoping that if Verity saw tonight's recording, she'd finally visit him. He was growing impatient, and his body was less willing to wait to enjoy her lush body now that he knew she was almost ready for him.

Knox let his head fall back against the metal headrest, focusing on the pain to keep him grounded in the present instead of falling prey to another fantasy. He needed to keep his wits about him because he wouldn't put it past the general to pay a late-night visit in hopes of catching him off guard. If that happened, it would be best if he wasn't clearly aroused by thoughts of his daughter.

He bit his lip where Verity had in his dream and tasted blood. His body had clearly attempted to recreate as many of the sensations as possible on its alone.

He had to wonder if Verity was still having similar dreams about him. She certainly had on his ship. He smiled, remembering watching that recording with much enjoyment. Aerue hadn't approved when he'd kicked the other guards out of the security station at the time. He was certain his friend would disapprove of his own explicit dreams.

In an instant, he was grounded back in reality. He heard the footsteps approaching again and recognized Verity's father even in the low-light.

To his surprise, none of the overhead bulbs illuminated. He doubted the general could see him well but perhaps he thought his presence would be more intimidating in the dark. It's not as if the human knew that Eochronians had pretty effective night vision thanks to seeing infrared heat signatures, and Knox was wearing his helmet which allowed him to distinguish the man's facial features, too.

He was wearing a frown and Knox had to wonder how the man didn't have permanent lines on his face from the ever-present expression. Perhaps he smiled and laughed a lot in other situations, enough to counteract the downward wrinkles. But Knox couldn't imagine the large man being happy. Maybe when Verity was born, but given she was a scientific experiment, he wondered how much of his joy would have been paternal joy and enthusiasm for his research.

"Did I disturb your sleep, Your Highness?" His voice dripped with so much disdain it felt like the air was clogged with it.

Knox stared blankly at him. What was the point of this late visit? "No," he answered truthfully.

"Are you nocturnal?"

Knox shrugged. "We measure time differently than humans. It's hard to say." It was true and it didn't tip his hand too much. He didn't want the general getting the idea that sleep deprivation would weaken him.

If their positions were switched, he would take any advantage offered to him and he was sure this human was the same. He embodied a militant personality beyond just being a general in his country's military force. Every time he saw the man, he wanted to pick a fight. Though he was sure that was at least partly based in the adversarial introduction they'd had when his soldiers had incapacitated him in their pursuit of capturing Verity.

Knox resisted the urge to shift in his seat again at the thought of her. He did not want to invite the general to the other side of the glass by giving him a reason to hit him again.

"My daughter went to see Dr. Lane again today because she's still sick. She left her protection detail to talk to you because she thought you knew why and would tell her. But you weren't any help."

Knox wondered if that meant she had told her father exactly

what he'd said or if she just omitted his answer altogether since it didn't provide information on her current condition.

He hadn't lied to her when he'd said he didn't know why she was reacting the way she was but any information he might have also shared with her was also interrupted by the arrival of the guards and his subsequent imprisonment.

Knox knew stating that fact would only further offend the general, though, because the man would likely take it as an attack on his protection of Verity.

A sound distracted him momentarily. The omnipresent noise of the cameras was now gone. Abruptly leaving silence in their wake. They'd been shut off. Because he was about to be tortured? But they'd been rolling earlier that day when the general had laid into him with his fists.

What was different now?

Though the change only confirmed that the cameras were indeed equipped with night vision. If he decided to make his escape under the cover of darkness, he'd still have to use his Eochronian skills and technology to avoid being detected too soon.

The man walked closer to the glass but still kept his distance unlike the dream version of his daughter. "I need to know exactly what you did to my daughter."

"I'm sure you can already imagine," he replied in an even voice.

The general's expression hardened even more, though Knox hadn't been sure that was possible.

"Believe me. If I punished you based on what I assumed, you'd be dead by dawn. Talking can only serve to save yourself from the multiple deaths I've been fantasizing about. Don't give me a reason to make them a reality."

Knox had no illusions that no matter what he said and once the general was able to convince everyone his usefulness was exhausted that he'd still be subjected to one of those gruesome fates. If he weren't planning on escaping long before it could be implemented.

Knox waited to see if the man's anger would prompt him to come closer or do something rash. Both men stared at each other in an impasse.

"No more than what you've already done," he finally answered.

Hatred flared in the general's eyes and he finally came closer.

If Knox were to break out of his prison now, he could easily overpower the man who now stood directly in his way. He wouldn't do either, of course, but he still cataloged the opportunity. Verity's father was proving over and over again that his daughter was his trigger and it was disappointingly easy to manipulate him by mentioning her.

Verity had been stronger against his mental manipulations and he wasn't going to insult her in her absence by assuming her resilience was due to her Eochronian DNA but merely her temperament. Her mother, again?

"Did you violate her?"

"No," he answered. He would have said more but offering a more in-depth explanation would lead to him either having to lie about whether he kissed her—and he didn't like directly lying if it were avoidable—or he would skirt the issue, undoubtedly drawing the human's sharp attention to the very thing he hoped to avoid.

Knox resisted the urge to yawn—from boredom not exhaustion—and leaned backward and got comfortable for what he assumed would be a long litany of questions.

10

VERITY

VERITY WOKE up sore and with a bad stomach ache. But it wasn't like the muscle aches of vomiting too much, or another wave of nausea, so it was progress. No, the knot currently sitting in her stomach was from anxiety. Over her current situation, her strange night, and having no idea what the future held.

McDonald hadn't been able to look her in the eye for the rest of the day yesterday after their second failed training session, and he hadn't woken her up early this morning to bring her to group fight training either.

She assumed her father had been told that they had switched to private sessions. That was the only reason he could possibly let her sleep in. She'd heard him leave sometime early in the morning and he hadn't returned but he could have easily woken her up with a phone call, or one of her guards could have knocked on her door in his stead. Regardless, Verity was glad for the extra sleep.

Verity got out of bed and quickly pulled on clothes. Since she was staying inside where they had been blasting air conditioning, she didn't have to worry about getting too sweaty in the summer heat. And since her return, she'd been feeling colder than usual.

She pulled a sweater on over her t-shirt and picked long lounge pants instead of shorts for the same reason.

She left her hair down. Hopefully McDonald would recognize it as proof she wasn't up for fight training today. Pulling it back into a ponytail took only a minute which only emphasized how out of it she felt.

McDonald glanced up and saw it was her before walking into the security room.

Flynn stayed at the kitchen table and handed her a glass of water.

She took it and sighed. Clearly, they had switched places as to who was her primary bodyguard.

Verity wondered if Flynn knew the real reason or if he had been told alternating was going to be part and parcel of the protection detail. She bet it was the latter. There was no way McDonald would risk word reaching her father's ears about what had happened. And that meant keeping the secret to themselves.

She accepted the glass. "Good morning, Flynn."

He smiled at her. "Late morning?"

"Couldn't sleep," she said.

"Nightmares?"

She nodded. Had he guessed because everyone knew nightmares accompanied people with trauma? Or did he have them to?

None of the STFs here had ever actually dealt with combat until the night she was abducted. And since then, she assumed they were similarly on edge like her. Though, obviously not in the same way. They hadn't been kidnapped the first time and had no expectation of it happening again.

Knox was the enemy for kidnapping her and the other humans, even if he hadn't barged through her front door himself. But for some reason, the title didn't seem to fit him like it clearly did the asshole Eiz'm.

But she knew there were enemies who worked through deception and backstabbing more than a frontal assault. Trohm was more than proof of that, on top of friends she'd had at school who would give someone a smile and then spread rumors the moment their back was turned.

But that didn't seem to fit him either. Because despite her father and Ben insisting that Knox had been lying to her this whole time, she still believed her instincts that told her he'd never directly deceived her.

Maybe she was a sucker for believing that, but only time would tell.

And with Knox now being held captive on base, she assumed that time would be coming sooner rather than later.

The idea of seeing him again made the pit in her stomach tighten. She raced back upstairs and took another one of the pills to avoid an episode.

She heard Flynn in the hallway and practically ran into him on the way back out of her room.

"You puke again?"

She shook her head. "Were you going to hold my hair?"

He nodded and she smiled.

"That's good to know." She walked toward the security room. "I'm going to watch some recordings."

She knew McDonald was there but like Hughes yesterday, she was expecting him to ignore her while they watched different monitors with their backs to each other. Hopefully that would minimize the awkwardness between them.

Flynn nodded and took up a spot near the back entrance of the house to cover what could be a vulnerability point for an intruder to take advantage of.

Verity walked into the room and took up her same spot from yesterday after giving a quick nod to McDonald. He returned it but still refused to look her in the eye.

She sighed. They'd have to get past this soon before her father noticed and demanded an explanation.

This time, Dr. Lane was visiting Knox alone and stood with her back to the camera for most of the recording.

Verity could see she was doing something with her hands and since Knox hadn't yet made a break for it, she assumed she wasn't unlocking the alien king. Besides, her arms were lifted which meant she was doing something around his head where there weren't any specific restraints on his forehead.

Her only guess was she was measuring him the same way volunteers in places with malnourished children would measure a child's wrist and head to measure the severity of a case.

But she couldn't see anything else happening in the video. So, why was her instinct telling her to keep watching?

But she wasn't scrutinizing Knox like she normally did. No, she was watching Dr. Lane.

Again, nothing made sense but Verity felt like she was seeing Dr. Lane in a new light.

Not literally, of course. There weren't any weird visual aberrations around the woman, or the tell-tale iridescent alien sheen that she'd seen on Knox—and herself, if her eyes were to be believed.

Verity closed the recording and walked back up to her room where she began to pace.

Was she being paranoid? Maybe.

But she had learned the hard way that being wary of threats wasn't enough to protect you from those threats. But she also agreed with Dr. Hudson that being irrationally and intensely afraid all the time wasn't a good way to live.

She lay down and stared up at the ceiling, then turned and stared at the pill bottle on her bedside table. She'd already taken one so there wasn't anything she could do about that—aside from forcing herself to throw up which wasn't an option she was willing to take. But she *could* stop taking the medicine now that she was doubting its source.

It wasn't much, but it was a plan.

Dr. Hudson was regularly impressing the importance of taking things one step at a time, and that's exactly what she was going to do.

VERITY WAITED until her father sat down at the table with her before she spoke up. She hadn't expected him to share dinner with her, but she was lucky tonight.

While she had decided against asking Dr. Hudson if she was letting paranoia get to her, she still wanted to tell her father her suspicions about Dr. Lane. He normally demanded evidence for her cases, like the college discussion prior to her abduction and the short-lived return. But he also respected gut feelings and had always told her to trust her instincts above all else.

He caught her staring and asked, "What?"

"I watched the footage of Dr. Lane's visit to Kn—the prisoner," she corrected.

"And?"

"Something feels off."

"How so?"

"We had no idea about Tristan, but I just have this feeling about Dr. Lane."

He raised an eyebrow and continued eating.

She thought he was effectively shutting down the conversation until he spoke again.

"When did this start?"

"Just watching the video. I've never felt it when talking to her in person." Aside from her sharing her test results with her father and Zeph *way* too soon for her to have obtained them. That still struck her as weird but her father had passed on Dr. Lane's explanation and it made enough sense that she had accepted it.

Maybe she shouldn't have. Because it was only further evidence of her off-feeling about her long-time doctor.

"What do you want to do about it?"

She shrugged. In the hours between her first consideration and his return, she still hadn't thought that far. Not for lack of trying, but she still had no answer.

"Do you want to stop seeing her? She's the most familiar with your history but she could hand it off to someone else in the practice if you want. It might take some time, though."

Verity took a bite of the lemon chicken on her plate and toyed with the option. It was a reasonable solution for anyone who didn't like their doctor, but she was concerned hers was an alien mole. And there was no guarantee that there wasn't another mole in the practice. For all she knew, her new doctor could be as shady as Dr. Lane was now in her mind. And if that turned out to be the case, the switch would be rendered pointless.

"Not yet," she said. She didn't mention her specific concerns but if her father asked for them, she'd give them. Based on the furrow between his eyebrows, she assumed he was already thinking along the same lines as her.

They ate the rest of the meal in silence, and it did nothing to make her feel better about the situation.

Verity knew she could be wrong about Dr. Lane and the medicine, but it was safest to proceed as if she had gotten irrefutable confirmation. She'd started feeling nauseated once the sun had set, but she was wary of taking another pill.

At some level, she knew that people took medicine all the time without thoroughly knowing all the ingredients. She was one of those people. But no one else on Earth was worried about their medicine secretly transforming them into some human-alien hybrid in the name of a nebulous and obscured alien science experiment. Knox had insisted he didn't want to conquer the planet, and she was pretty sure Eiz'm wanted to, but being a lab rat for even a beneficial study brought up some weird questions. She'd had some friends use her for psych projects, and it was always a little strange to know you were being reduced to certain results—even more so than the testing grades necessary for college admission.

And in this case, she hadn't been asked to consent to her participation in the study. Her father had signed her up when she was a baby and then the aliens had taken it one step further.

But if the medicine could make her feel better, was it stupid stubbornness on her side to resist something she knew could help?

It wasn't as if she were dying of cancer and was willing to try an experimental treatment on the off chance she could live longer—if not cured. This was about how much she was willing to give up her humanity at the cost of suffering uncomfortable and strange symptoms. And for all she knew, resisting the change would eventually kill her, too. She had nothing to compare her experience to. No one did. And the only people she could ask were clearly biased.

Before she climbed into bed, she moved the pill bottle to her desk. She wouldn't take another one tonight but maybe she'd change her mind in the morning. She stared at it from under the covers and went to sleep with the important question still weighing on her.

11

KNOX

KNOX CLICKED the incoming message on his wrist and watched the Eochronian letters flash across his helmet's visor in quick succession. It was about a rate of one per second, too fast for anyone not fluent in the language to track and memorize the message as it was laid out.

It was from Dr. Makzik, though why she wasn't directly speaking to him or even through video communication, he had no idea.

VERITY DECLINING, it read. STOPPED MEDICATION.

Knox frowned. She hadn't resumed her treatment for long enough that her stopping it again would cause withdrawal. Then again, she had proven to be very sensitive to the Eochronian agents in her body.

But he also hadn't been told she'd made another visit to Dr. Makzik to let her know she had stopped taking the pills. Had she successfully tagged Verity with a listening device? And if she had, why wasn't he aware of it?

He drew his response on his wrist. LISTENING DEVICE?

GUARD.

Ah, that made more sense.

SEND UPDATES, he wrote back.

If Verity was declining at such a rapid pace, however, he needed to leave sooner rather than later just to take care of her. His timeline was more dependent on her than he wanted to admit, but if her wellbeing was in jeopardy, he'd have to postpone the project even more. She was vital to its success, and needed to be healthy for it to work out. His personal priorities may have flipped, with her meaning more than just a part of his plan, but they were both still interconnected. Eiz'm and some of his kind might believe he had completely forsaken the original goal, being too wrapped up in the fascinating human, but he hadn't. The program was still very much in play, but they couldn't move forward on it without her.

He turned to the cameras and spoke loudly. "Verity, I can help you. Just come talk to me."

Even if she didn't see it herself, he was certain someone would eventually pass the message along.

He was done doing nothing while he waited for her to come to him. If she didn't show up soon, he'd go to her. Hell with letting the humans believe they'd subdued him. He wouldn't let her die when he knew he could help her.

And while her father may hate him for what had happened before, he knew the general wouldn't begrudge him saving her life.

12

VERITY

VERITY PAUSED in the doorway of the makeshift security room.

Her father was sitting in her normal spot and was glaring at the screen.

She stepped closer, being sure to stay as quiet as possible.

Hughes turned to greet her but she gave a silent nod instead, which he thankfully returned before turning back to the screens in front of him.

That's when she saw the confirmation box pop open asking him if he was certain he wanted to continue with the deletion.

"What are you deleting?" she asked.

Her father's shoulders tensed but he luckily didn't click CONFIRM. He turned to her. "How long were you standing there?"

"Just a few seconds."

"I didn't even hear you come downstairs."

That part had been kind of obvious.

"So?" she prompted. "What are you deleting?"

Instead of answering, he got up from the seat and left, calling over his shoulder, "I'll be back late tonight. Don't wait up."

She hadn't been planning on it, but now she was almost tempted to. Just to confront him about why he was acting like an overgrown toddler. A description she'd never thought would apply to her level-headed and mature-beyond-his-years father.

She filled his seat and clicked no so she could see the file her father had been about to delete.

It was a recording from last night.

Knox was alone without any visitors, but he was talking directly to the camera. And asking to see her, promising to help her.

She paused the video and stared at his expression.

He looked and sounded earnest but even from this distance she could tell there was an ulterior motive shining in his hypnotic eyes.

She stood up and tapped Hughes on his shoulder.

He turned in the chair to face her. "Yes?"

"I need to visit the prisoner."

"I'm not allowed to take you to see him."

"He asked to see me directly."

"Your father gave us instructions at the start of the detail—"

"If you don't come with me, I'll go on my own."

He sighed and gave her a glare she assumed a big brother would give to an annoying little sister. She didn't care. She needed to see Knox again, and now was the perfect time since she had stopped the medicine and wasn't in the middle of an episode. Because who knew how long that would last?

She didn't she didn't want her line of questioning to be undercut by her suddenly emptying her stomach onto her shoes. Talk about unprofessional.

Verity watched Hughes press a finger to his earwig as he filled McDonald and the rest of her protection detail about her plan.

Thanks to her enhanced senses, she could hear McDonald on the other side saying it wasn't a good idea but that if she was insistent to not let her out of Hughes' sight.

Verity rolled her eyes.

She couldn't blame McDonald's words of advice, but it wasn't really staying in her guards' sights that was the problem in her father's eyes. It was her having any continued contact with the aliens who had tortured her and held her captive.

She'd told the truth about what they'd done to her to Special Agent Kaur, but her father wasn't an idiot and obviously sensed she'd held things back.

His imagination was probably running wild, assuming they had done even worse to her than reality. She could tell him and put him out of his misery but if she did, she knew he'd probably kill Knox anyway.

And she hadn't yet been able to stamp out the small and insistent part of her that still cared about the alien king. Things would be so much simpler if she didn't, but it seemed she'd never be lucky where he was concerned.

Hughes finally finished the conversation.

One of the guards from outside came in, and the men switched places.

"Clear?" Hughes asked into his mic.

She heard the affirmative answer and then Hughes pulled open the front door and ushered her through.

Together, they walked quickly to the prison building.

Verity wondered if her father was in his office or if he was visiting Knox right now. If she ran into him there, it would be a little awkward, but she wouldn't let his presence stop her from getting the answers she needed.

The guards closed the gap between them, making it impossible for her to reach the door.

"He asked to see me."

They didn't move. "The general was very clear you weren't allowed to be here, Miss Landau," one of the older men said.

She rubbed the back of her neck in frustration, her hand coming away with sweat courtesy of the summer sun.

"Please let me in," she said again. "I'll get him talking."

They moved aside without protest, as if they'd only been

waiting for the magic word. But she knew better. She didn't question it and watched Hughes enter the code.

It was different than the last time and she had no illusions about why that was the case.

Together, they descended the stairs and entered the basement.

"Wait here," she told Hughes once they were at the door.

"I can't protect you from a separate room," he objected.

"He'd have to go through you to take me out of here, Hughes. I don't want anything to happen to you."

He held her gaze in a staring contest but looked away first at the veiled mention of Harrison and Ben's deaths.

She took a deep breath and forced herself to keep talking. "I'm going to be on the other side of the glass from him. I'm not asking you to stay across the base while I talk to him alone. Just on this side of the door. If something goes wrong, you can burst through it and save me in no time."

Her guard frowned but finally opened the metal barrier for her.

Verity blinked, entering the garishly bright hallway. Ugh, that was torture alone. If she got a migraine from this, she was going to be pissed. At least it wasn't a strobe light.

Her father was nowhere to be seen, which was a blessing she was very grateful for.

As she strolled down the corridor, she had the distinct feeling that she was Clarice in Silence of the Lambs on her way to meet Hannibal Lector. She just hoped she didn't end up in the same messed-up relationship they did by the third book where Clarice also became a cannibal.

She repressed her gag reflex. She shouldn't have thought of that. Even the mysterious medicine wasn't enough to get that awful image out of her mind.

But the comparison still stood because there was Knox, sitting behind a thick glass panel watching her with an intensity she felt even with so much distance between them.

"You came," he said.

She walked closer. "Did you doubt that I would?"

"I wasn't certain you'd get the message."

"I almost didn't."

He smiled. "Your father?"

She nodded. But she refused to say more. She wasn't about to gossip about her father with him. He'd turn it to his advantage somehow, and she wasn't about to hand him ammunition.

"You said you could help me."

"So, you admit you need it?"

She narrowed her eyes.

"Don't get mad, Verity. I only ask because I wasn't sure you would. I assume you pride yourself on your self-sufficiency."

She crossed her arms, needing some shield against him. He knew her too well. "Well?" she demanded.

"I heard you're feeling sick again after stopping your medication."

How—?

"How many spies do you still have here?"

"If I told you, that would ruin their undercover status, wouldn't it?"

"Not really," she said. "Since you still wouldn't be telling us who they are."

He didn't reply, either to disagree or change the subject. Silence descended between them.

She glanced over her shoulder at the ceiling, searching for the cameras. She couldn't find them but she was sure they were recording every moment of this interaction. Even so, she took a step closer. Then another and another until she was only a foot away from the glass wall between them.

"You're the one who called me here. If you're not going to actually talk to me, I can leave."

He shifted slightly in his chair and Verity fought the instinct to retreat. Was he about to break out or was he going to continue the farce of his captivity until the conversation was over?

"How are you feeling right now?"

"Fine," she said. If you ignored her anxiety.

"Did you go back on the medicine?"

"You keep calling it medicine but we know that's not the case. So, why don't you cut the BS and call it what it is?"

He tilted his head, studying her. "And what is that?"

She hadn't even realized she abbreviated it. It's not like she censored herself with that word on a regular basis. Her classmates and her were no stranger to cursing and to the STFs on base, it was a second language for everyone. "It means bullshit."

He smiled. "I know what the abbreviation means. I'm asking what you think the pill is."

"Whatever you were giving me on your ship."

He raised an eyebrow but didn't deny her assumption, which meant she was right and he didn't want a record of him admitting to experimenting on her.

"So, you clearly have someone here on Earth to finish the job." The question was whether she was right about Dr. Lane or if the person filling the prescription had pulled the switch without her doctor knowing.

Either scenario wasn't good for her, but it could exonerate her long-time doctor.

"Was there a question in there, Verity?" He almost sounded bored.

Which was the only reason she took another step forward. Even as she did it, she knew it was a mistake. And his smile only confirmed it.

"That's not why I asked you here."

"You got me here under false pretenses. Why am I not surprised?"

"Well, the answer to you feeling better is obviously to continue taking the pills."

Not the answer she'd been hoping for but a part of her had expected it.

"Of course, it would be even better if you came back with me and Dr. Mak'en could directly treat you to monitor your side effects."

She gave him what she hoped was a clearly fake smile. "Of course," she echoed. "But if my well-being isn't why you actually called me here, then what else do you want to talk about?"

"Who says I want to talk?"

Verity couldn't stop the hot flush that swept her from head to toe at his lascivious tone and infuriatingly attractive smile.

She needed to remember he was an alien drawing her human self in like wild predators did to their unsuspecting prey. It only made it worse that she *knew* it was happening but wasn't able to effectively fight it.

She almost wished he'd just grab her now so she wasn't anxious about when he'd make his next move.

"Eiz'm is causing trouble."

Why wasn't she surprised?

She crossed her arms and asked, "And, how is that my problem?"

Knox leaned forward. "Given he wants to violently conquer your planet, I think it would be quite obvious."

She frowned. "And you don't?"

"I've always insisted you were wrong about my intentions."

"You have."

"Does that mean you believe me?"

"Don't put words in my mouth."

"So, what can I?"

"Nothing," she replied, her tone biting. He'd already given her food which she had been almost positive was laced with something and if he was accidentally or intentionally making a sexual innuendo, she wasn't going to encourage him. She crossed her arms. "So, he wants to take over Earth. I kinda already knew that. There's got to be more you haven't told me yet."

"He's teamed up with our old enemies to form a personal army."

That didn't sound good but Verity forced her voice to sound bored. "And?"

"They're bigger and more sturdy fighters than my kind."

Well, shit. It was already hard enough to fight one of Knox's. The fact that she'd been able to on her escape was probably a product of her adrenaline and likely a command to go easy on her from their king. She had already fought two when they kidnapped her but her resistance had seemed to surprise them and she had ultimately lost that fight. Had they been going at her full-throttle, she was almost positive she wouldn't have gotten two steps away from the dining table that night.

"So… they're different from you?"

He nodded. "More brawn than brains."

"Are you saying you're more brains than brawn?"

"Nope. That's a different one of our enemies. We're blessed with equal brains and brawn."

"But superior to humans."

He smiled.

"So… do I call you Alien Race A, B, and C, or do you actually have species names so I can keep this all straight in my head?"

"The Vruxols have aligned with Eiz'm. I'm the king of the Eochronians, and thankfully the Lielneh have decided to sit this conflict out."

"Would really suck for you if all your enemies teamed up."

"Would suck for you, too, in this situation."

As if she could forget.

13

KNOX

KNOX LEANED FORWARD to watch Verity pull out her phone. She hesitated only a moment before answering an incoming call.

"Hello," she answered.

The general's voice boomed on the other end. "What the hell do you think you're doing?"

He couldn't contain the chuckle at the man's impotent anger when it came to controlling his daughter.

She shot him a glare and turned her back to him so he couldn't read her facial expressions as he blatantly eavesdropped on her conversation.

She was getting—chewed out, he believed was the term—for what probably wouldn't be the last time for her disobedience.

Verity had told him that she respected authority while they were on his ship. Either she had been lying or that deference didn't extend to her father.

He heard her long intake of breath and watched her back and shoulder muscles contract underneath her shirt before relaxing.

Her next words surprised him as much as her father.

"We need to release him."

He sat up straighter, trying to see a glimpse of her expression but she was resolutely keeping her face turned away.

Her father shouted, "Are you crazy?"

"I know." She started pacing back and forth in front of him, finally giving him her profile to admire. "I can't believe I'm saying it either. But we have bigger problems. There's an alien army on its way. And if he's out of jail, he might be able to help us."

"He's their leader."

"He didn't order the impending attack."

"How do you know?"

"Because he doesn't want to conquer the Earth," She looked at Knox, and he flashed a smile, "...with violence," she finished.

She flushed but didn't otherwise respond.

"Then what is his plan?" the general demanded.

"He's right there, Dad. I can put him on speaker and you can ask him."

"I don't trust him."

Nor should he.

Verity finally turned to fully face him again. She took a step forward again and held the phone up to the glass.

He tilted his head. What was she expecting him to say? He wasn't about to beg for his freedom. Her father would deny it just on principle if he did. Besides, he didn't know what Verity's plan was. Releasing him wasn't necessary to gain his help against Eiz'm but he wasn't about to abort her campaign.

If he never had to show his hand by breaking out because she released him first, it would be all the better. And now he was curious to learn what she had planned for him.

Another flip of their original situation but he wasn't going to complain if it meant he finally got to spend more time with her. He could grab her and return to space whenever he wanted, especially if he was about to be removed from this awful metal chair.

He heard the general ask, "Verity?"

When Knox didn't say anything, she put the phone to her ear again. "I'm still here, Dad. Hughes is just outside the door. I really think releasing him would be the best option."

"Not without contingencies."

"What would you suggest?"

"I'll be there in ten. Do *not* do anything stupid, Verity, do you hear me? Stay where you are and stay away from the glass."

Instead of answering, she hung up and sat on the ground, apparently making herself comfortable for the interim until her father arrived.

She sat with her legs crossed in front of her and tapped something on her phone before putting it down.

He heard the tell-tale sound of another recording happening. Interesting that she did it *now* after she'd already asked him the important questions.

And since they both knew the room was being monitored it seemed a little redundant. Perhaps she planned to listen to the recording privately and didn't want anyone else to have access to it?

"What do we do now?" he asked.

"We wait."

"In silence?"

"Do you have a problem with that?"

Not normally, but he liked hearing her voice, even when it was throwing barbs at him.

"How do you know about the attack if you've been stuck here?"

"I knew before you laid the trap for me." He knew it wasn't strictly true from the listening devices he'd planted on the guards but he wanted to hear how she'd try to spin it.

"It wasn't me," she admitted, surprising him with the truth.

"But you were the bait."

She didn't deny it.

"What? I don't get an apology for you ruthlessly seducing me as means to an end?"

"I think you owe me one first."

"I'm sorry for how we met."

"That's not what I meant."

He wasn't going to apologize for her getting involved in his plan because he didn't regret anything that led to their meeting.

"You're not going to apologize for kidnapping me, then? And using me as a lab rat?"

He wondered if she had demanded an apology from her father on that score, too.

"As I'm not the one who broke into your house that night, I'm not technically the one who kidnapped you."

"They were acting on your orders. That makes you as guilty as them, if not more, Knox."

She said his name like a curse but he still smiled at hearing her say it after all this time.

"I've never lied to you and I'm not going to start now, Verity."

She leaned back on her hands, an action that pressed her chest out in an enticing manner that he doubted she'd appreciate him noting. "What does that have to do with anything?"

"I'm not sorry we met, but I do apologize for the circumstances."

She sighed. "That's the best I'm going to get out of you, huh?"

"In that regard, yes, but I'm willing to give you other things."

"Do you ever think about anything other than sex?"

"In general or when I'm around you?"

She rolled her eyes.

"Because the answer is yes to both, though you take up most of my thoughts when we're together."

"Forget I asked."

"You sound disappointed."

"I said drop it, Knox."

But he wasn't done. "But I promise that I'd only be thinking of you when we finally get together."

She glared at him. "I'm only interested in information, so keep it in your pants."

"I'm tied up, Verity. I can't do much of anything right now unless you want to remedy the situation."

"I already am, remember? You're getting released."

"I doubt your father is going to let me go so easily. And does that mean you're not interested in me? Because then I'd have to call you a liar. You've already lied to me before."

"No, I haven't," she responded.

"Oh. So, our last dinner before your escape was what, exactly?"

She sat up straight. "A diversion. That's different than lying."

Before she answered, there was a sound on the door before it opened and five men entered with her father. He assumed one was Verity's personal guard given his different outfit from the other three.

General Landau ran in, his gun drawn and aimed at Knox, despite the glass barrier between them.

Verity cleared her throat, drawing the attention of the men.

Knox assumed they had seen her but in their panic, hadn't fully registered that her presence meant that she was alive and well.

The man couldn't mask his surprise before Knox caught it.

Perhaps the man had been expecting to see an empty room due to his daughter being abducted again.

It was a reasonable assumption to have. Had Verity not advocated for releasing him, that had been Knox's plan.

Verity's father jerked his chin towards the wall and the four uniformed guards walked through the door.

Knox listened to their synchronized steps and heard them file through the hidden passageway that led to his side of the glass.

The door opened behind him and two of the guards grabbed

his arms as they started undoing his restraints while the third went to work on his feet.

The fourth stood behind him and attached a band around his neck that beeped shut.

Knox rolled his head, testing the mobility the new accessory afforded him.

He noted how Verity's eyes were glued to his neck.

"What is that?" she asked her father.

The man pulled a remote out of his pocket and pressed a button.

Knox held in a curse as an unpleasant shock shot through his body.

"Shock collar," the general answered.

How demeaning. It wasn't as painful as the human probably hoped but it wasn't a fun sensation either. A part of him wished Verity had control of it because he doubted she'd abuse its power. Then again, she would probably be tempted to use it every time he annoyed her—even when he wasn't trying to. An impartial third party would be the best option but he doubted General Landau would be sacrificing control of it to anyone, not even his daughter.

Once he was finally free of the chair, his hands were bound behind his back in cuffs and the four guards surrounded him. They escorted him to where Verity and the general were waiting for him.

"Where is he going to stay?" she asked, eyeing him with a healthy amount of distrust though he noticed her eyes did leisurely wander the length of his body.

Knox pressed his shoulders back and she looked away with a blush that her father seemed to catch based on the death glare the man shot him.

"With us?" she asked.

Her tone was uncertain and he wasn't sure if she wanted that to be the case or if she was worried about that potential arrangement.

"Over my dead body," her father growled. "He'll be staying in the medical building where Dr. Lane can conduct her tests without interruption."

He saw Verity's shoulders drop with relief but she still didn't fully relax.

What he wouldn't give to see her genuinely comfortable around him. Her plan for them to spend more time together had clearly been overruled by her father so perhaps he'd spirit her away soon, after all.

14

VERITY

VERITY COULDN'T HELP but smile in response to Dr. Lane's surprised expression when she and her father brought Knox in. She still didn't have enough evidence to go to her father with her suspicions, but she was keeping her eye out for anything to support her case. If she was right and the woman was really an alien, Verity was impressed by her acting chops.

Dr. Lane had recovered relatively quickly and addressed her father. "General Landau, is there something I can help you with?"

"We've decided to relocate the prisoner here to better support your research efforts. He will be here under guard for you and your staff's protection. If there are any problems, you have my direct number."

"Of course, General."

She addressed the four guards who were still holding Knox. "If you'd follow me, please."

Verity took a step to do so but her father held her back.

"You're going home," he said.

Hughes stepped forward.

She turned on her heel and followed the man out without

another word. She wasn't going to beg her father to let her stay, but him treating her like a little girl was getting really old.

The elevator doors opened but before she stepped inside, her father's voice rang out.

"Special Agent Kaur will be visiting you later this afternoon with more questions. I won't be able to make it but I expect your full cooperation and honesty in your answers."

She didn't bother answering and let the elevator door close behind her.

Hughes was silently staring at the door and she watched the numbers descend as always.

"How much trouble are you in with my dad?"

He made a small, dissatisfied sound but didn't say anything.

"I'll talk to him about it."

"That won't be necessary, ma'am."

"It's Verity," she corrected.

He didn't acknowledge she'd spoken.

Verity let it go. If he didn't want her to help smooth things over with her dad, then fine. He was a grown man and could clearly take whatever punishment her father had decided to hand out.

She really needed to patch things up with McDonald though. Especially now that her father knew that Hughes had swapped roles with him as her main guard. She didn't want McDonald getting in trouble for that.

McDonald was waiting for them at the door when they arrived home. He nodded at Hughes and the latter walked right into the security room, leaving her and McDonald in the foyer.

"Are you in trouble?" she asked.

"Are you?" he returned.

"That bad?" she asked.

He shrugged. "Look, I'm sorry for avoiding you. No hurt feelings?"

She smiled and held out her hand. "No harm, no foul."

He shook it and she immediately felt the tension between them disappear.

Now that Ben was gone, he was the closest thing she had to a friend on base, and she was glad to be back on speaking terms with him.

"So… you spoke to him?" McDonald asked, as they walked into the kitchen where he poured and handed her a glass of water.

She took it and tipped it in a silent thank you. She took a long sip, buying time before she'd have to answer his eager questions.

She swallowed and put the glass down on the counter. "Yes," she sighed.

"And?"

"He wasn't that helpful about why I've been sick, but he did say an alien invasion is coming soon." Which was obviously extremely valuable information.

"He just volunteered that news? What did he say? 'Oh, by the way, my kind is going to attack you. Thought you should know.'"

She knew he was being facetious but she nodded anyway.

McDonald crossed his arms. "And you trust him?"

"Given it's spearheaded by someone who has a history of going against him and hates his guts, it makes sense."

"What if he's playing you?"

"Possibly," she admitted. But she still highly doubted it. "Doesn't really matter at this point, though. Besides, he could have kidnapped me the moment I stepped into the building." Or even while she was sleeping at night, but she didn't say that. She didn't want McDonald and Hughes becoming any more hyper-attentive to her every move.

Besides, the people on the base were already on high alert. Telling them that all their precautions were probably pointless wouldn't do much except make everyone unbearable and point-lessly paranoid. As Dr. Hudson told her, being worried about one's safety was an important part of survival but being so hyperaware for prolonged periods of time without a true threat being present did more harm than good to the human body.

"Did my dad tell you that a special agent will be coming to question me later today?"

McDonald nodded. "He did. Some jerk named Agent Smith, right?"

She smiled at his pop culture reference. "Special Agent Kaur, but close enough," she replied.

"Want one of us in the room?"

She shook her head. "I don't think he's an alien mole." Though she obviously hadn't been good at spotting Trohm. Then again, she hadn't known aliens were real at that point so she wasn't going to beat herself up TOO much over that particular failure. "You can just wait outside an open door."

"I'll wait inside the door with you," he said.

She shrugged. Worked for her. She wasn't going to tell Kaur anything she didn't feel comfortable saying to McDonald or any of the other guards. No matter what she said to anyone, it would eventually get to her father, so that was the only thing that was determining what she would keep to herself.

The annoying man hadn't visited Knox again since the first recorded interrogation she'd seen but she doubted Knox was sharing their more personal interactions, either. Probably for the same reason, too—avoiding her father's ire.

In that, they were united.

"So, did my father let you know when he was stopping by?"

McDonald checked his watch. "In two hours."

Ugh. Forever would be too soon to see him again. "I'm going upstairs to take a nap." The adrenaline from seeing Knox was starting to wear off and she wanted to be at peak mental alertness when she had to square off with Kaur again.

.   .   .

VERITY WOKE up before her alarm went off, a strange sensation prickling over her skin.

She threw off the covers and checked her mirror again but didn't see anything unusual in her reflection except a slightly crazed look in her eyes. Looking closer, it looked like they had become a darker brown but even stranger that gold flecks were starting to appear in her irises. Another change? Or was she grasping at straws?

A sound downstairs drew her attention and she ran down to the first floor while finger-combing her hair. She hated the Special Agent but she didn't want to give him another reason to look down on her.

But he wasn't the cause of the commotion.

The moment she reached the first floor, she was face to face with Knox, who was smiling up at her as if he were her prom date.

His four guards were missing, which meant he was standing alone and free of anything that could obstruct his motion. At least, that's what she could see apart from his hands being held behind his back. If he was still wearing cuffs, she knew he could break through them easily. Had he come to kidnap her again?

There was only one reason his guards would be gone in reality: if they were dead. But Knox kept insisting he hadn't killed any humans and she was starting to believe him. Was it because she trusted him or his repetition had successfully brainwashed her?

Which meant this had to be a dream—right?

Someone coughed and she looked over to see McDonald standing to the side, his arms crossed like a protective older brother.

There was no way she'd dream about him, so this had to be real, after all.

"What are you doing here?" she demanded of the alien king. It was so strange seeing him in her home, as if it were a normal occurrence.

"I'm supposed to be interrogated by the human agent."

That still didn't explain why he was standing in her home. Unless they were going to be questioned together? Did her dad know? How the hell had he gotten his guards to go along with this if her father wasn't in the loop to issue orders?

"He's not very pleasant to be around, is he?" he continued.

She nodded in agreement but her mind was back on wondering why he was alone. "Where are your guards?"

He tilted his head towards the security room.

She frowned. Not because she thought he was lying but because it still made no sense that only McDonald was physically present with her and Knox. Everyone on base knew what Knox was capable of—by proxy of whoever had framed him for the murders, if you believed him—so why wasn't he being watched closely in her home? Was one of the guards another spy of his who had managed to talk the rest of the detail into becoming lax?

"You look nervous," he said, drawing her attention back to him. "Are you okay?"

She forced a smile. "Fine." She walked past him and McDonald toward the kitchen, ignoring the heat of their stares on her.

But this time, only one was checking her out. The STF wasn't playing right now and that meant he probably only had eyes for the enemy, not her unless it was to make sure she was safe.

Verity pulled down another glass for herself, not wanting to run back upstairs to grab the one she'd left by her bed. She didn't trust the guys to behave if she was gone even for a moment.

She pulled down two extras and filled them. She put a straw into one so it could be consumed. She held them out to McDonald and Knox.

Her guard refused the offer. He probably didn't want to diminish his reaction time by having something in his hands but if he wasn't careful, he'd end up dehydrated. Once Knox was gone, she was going to make sure he actually drank something.

Her unexpected visitor accepted it with a smile. With his hand, which meant he hadn't been cuffed this whole time. She resisted the urge to flinch at the electric jolt she felt when his fingers closed over hers. When she was sure he had a solid grasp on it, she let go and grabbed her own.

They both took a long drink, watching each other over the rims of their glasses. It brought her back to their first meal together and when she took his glass of the fancy ambrosia-like drink.

He hadn't been able to hide his lustful interest in her when she'd done that and thinking of it now made her cheeks heat.

His eyes darkened, and she guessed he was remembering the same thing as her.

She finished her sip and forced herself to swallow around the lump in her throat.

She checked the clock on the wall and almost sighed with relief. Special Agent Douche should be arriving any moment and hopefully his stupid presence and sexist attitude would help cut the tension between her and Knox. Triangulating, as she'd learned from watching an online video about couple counseling. *Not* that she and Knox were a couple. Regardless of what any of the men in her life thought, she refused to be paired off with the confusing and infuriating alien king. As if he could sense the concerning direction her thoughts had taken, he smirked at her and took another sip of water as if it were the same life-saving element for his kind—Eochronians, now that she had a name for them—as it was for humanity.

If Eiz'm or Knox's more sneaky and still secret plan for Earth succeeded—and there was a frightening chance that would be the outcome of everything—she hoped that any surviving humans wouldn't die of thirst. She'd read a novel about that and it was *not* something she wanted to experience for real. Then again, she'd survived an alien abduction so maybe she'd be better at handling it than she assumed.

She glared at him, and then the clock again. Where was Special Agent Kaur when you needed him?

There was a thought she never expected to have. But it was just more proof that she had the absolute worst luck when it came to Knox.

15

KNOX

KNOX KEPT his gaze on Verity but was starting to get irritated by her guard's constant death glare. He assumed if her captain were still alive, he'd be giving him the same expression. Knox couldn't blame him for redirecting his grief as fury but given he wasn't the actual murderer and wished Verity no harm, it was annoying to be an undeserving target.

He'd successfully convinced his guards to all but abandon their duties once he'd been brought into the house but he wasn't going to risk influencing Verity's right in front of her. No human had ever realized what he was doing before but he was sure that if anyone could, she would be the one to figure it out.

And he'd overheard her successful use of the skill earlier, talking the guards of his prison into letting her see him. Which finally answered his question about whether the hybrids would be able to. Perhaps lending his own DNA for the basis of his program had been a mistake. He didn't want everyone having the special power, though he assumed not many would recognize it for what it was.

Verity hadn't brought it up to him yet so either she didn't

know or didn't want to talk about it until they could have a truly private discussion. Which would be impossible as long as they were on the airbase. He was tempted to take her away now before the Special Agent could arrive but he was curious about what she'd say to the man with him close enough to overhear.

The doorbell rang, and he watched her guard's hand go straight to the weapon holstered at his hip. He drew it and pointed the barrel towards the front door with one hand while motioning Verity to move with his other.

She silently pressed her back to the wall without complaint, essentially hiding from an intruder's line of sight.

He didn't bother moving. He wouldn't need to rely on avoiding detection to win a fight against anyone here or outside.

Knox watched as one of the other guards from the security room went to the front door and slowly opened it. From his vantage point, he could easily recognize the agent and was both excited and irritated by his arrival.

"About time," the man complained as he was led into the living room.

Their eyes locked and the human failed to hide his surprise at his presence. Thankfully, Verity hadn't seen it or she would have quickly realized he had convinced his human handlers to bring them together to make it more convenient for the agent. At least, that was the excuse he'd given. Of course, he couldn't care less about the annoying human.

Verity's guard finally put away his weapon and ushered her out of the kitchen, keeping his body firmly between hers and Knox's. He followed behind them and sat next to Verity before anyone could object to the seating arrangement. She didn't react, refusing to spare him even a glance, but the agent lifted his eyebrow in silent curiosity as he regarded them together.

The man pulled out a recorder, pressed a button, and set it on the table next to him.

Out of the corner of his eye, Knox could see Verity glaring at the small device.

"This is Special Agent Kaur speaking to Verity Landau and... Knox," the man said, seeming incredulous at the scenario.

He couldn't blame the man for that, but Knox was sure it wouldn't be long before something came up.

"When did you first meet?"

Knox saw Verity tilt her head as she regarded the man. He could practically hear the snarky comment forming in her mind but she held her tongue.

Was it because it was being recorded by this man, specifically? It had to be. She had known that he was being watched in his cell and hadn't held back her usual attitude then. Or was it because she knew her father would eventually be listening to this recording, and HE was the true reason for her reticence?

Knox felt the vibrations as someone started to bounce their leg under the table. The source was surprisingly Verity. He slowly moved his hand over her thigh and rested it there.

She stilled immediately but didn't pull away from him. But now that her nervous energy didn't have a kinetic escape, he could feel the tension locking her muscles.

He could see the Special Agent's growing frustration at their continued silence. Knox didn't want to get shocked by the collar, and he wasn't certain how far the range was or whether Verity's overzealous guard was texting the general real-time updates, though he doubted it as the man had yet to come crashing through the front door. But cooperating in this silly exercise was probably the best way to stay on the humans' good side as much as possible, though he knew for a fact that potential was severely limited for certain individuals.

What was the saying? Beggars couldn't be choosers.

"My guards brought her to meet me," he answered.

Her spine snapped straight. Was she shocked he was sharing? Or was she apprehensive about what he was going to reveal?

Knox squeezed her thigh, hoping to reassure her that he wasn't about to share any truly personal details. He didn't want this human knowing those details, much less her father. He was certain she felt the same way, so at least in that matter, they were in agreement.

"Was she cooperative?"

Knox frowned. Of course she hadn't been, not that he blamed her. But why was the Special Agent now speaking as if she wasn't in the room? She might not be willing to share, but talking about her like an object without a care for her feelings was not okay.

"Why don't you ask her?" Knox answered, keeping his voice even.

The man shot him a frustrated look as if he had just betrayed some brotherhood by looping Verity back in.

She shifted in her chair and crossed her legs. But rather than her moving the leg he was holding, which he would have easily released had she given any indication that's what she wanted, she actually trapped his hand with the motion.

If she weren't always so mindful of her actions around him— and he was always aware that she was very measured in front of him except perhaps with her words which always seemed to express her instinctive reactions—he would wonder if she hadn't considered the outcome of the gesture. But since she had to be aware, he was now at a loss as to what her motivation was.

It wasn't as if she needed to distract him again like she had for her half-baked escape with her captain. They never would have succeeded without his intervention, though he wasn't about to share that particular detail with her. She'd probably slap him. But a part of him wondered if she was at least subconsciously aware of that fact.

"Were you cooperative?" the Special Agent asked, directing his question to her this time.

She made a little snort. "No, I did not *cooperate* with my

captors when they grabbed me in the middle of the night and forced me in front of their king for some perverted presentation ceremony."

He released his hand from her thigh, extricating it at the tone in her voice. She was really pissed, though he wasn't sure if it was the memory or who she was recounting it to. Either way, he didn't want to further aggravate her or be in striking distance when she eventually reached her breaking point, but he wasn't going to move away from her more than absolutely necessary when she was allowing him to be this close.

"How was he during your first meeting?"

Knox leaned back in his seat and waited for her answer.

"Polite," she said. "But I also thought he was arrogant."

The Special Agent glanced at him for confirmation. Knox shrugged. He wasn't about to deny it. He hadn't meant to come off as the latter though having the upper hand in that situation did lend a certain amount of self-assurance, and he could see how that would be interpreted as arrogance.

"You mentioned having meals together. Was he the same during those interactions?"

Verity shrugged but clearly wasn't going to verbally answer that question if her crossing her arms was any indication. She uncrossed and recrossed her legs in the opposite direction, turning her body slightly away from him.

A small chill seeped through him at the gesture despite the lack of cold air. He forced the sting of rejection away. It was irrational and was a pointless feeling.

Verity's move might not have anything to do with him. And if it did, there was nothing he could do about it.

Taking his hand back had clearly been the right choice. Still, he missed the physical contact with her. It had been too long since he'd last been treated to the privilege and luxury that he was clearly becoming a little obsessed with it.

Recognizing the dead end, the man turned his attention back to Knox for the next question.

The interview continued in the same manner. The questions weren't outright intrusive in most cases but whenever he or Verity refused an answer, the man switched his focus, and he seemed surprised and satisfied with the amount of information he was still getting.

When Special Agent Kaur finally turned off the recorder, Knox could feel Verity relax next to him even though he hadn't touched her again since the start of the interview.

Verity's other guard escorted the special agent out but neither she nor Knox made any move to leave the table even after he was gone.

If he couldn't see her breathing, he could have mistaken her for an inanimate double given how still she'd been for the last thirty minutes, since they'd started talking more about the experiments that had been done on her.

He'd still kept his answers to a minimum, not wanting to give any of the humans—Verity included—too much information about his project, but she had barely given any details.

She had to remember them, but maybe they were too upsetting for her to verbalize? He didn't like the thought of that. Aside from Eiz'm's abuse and the drowning incident which he was still furious about, he had thought they had taken pretty good care of her. Had he been wrong? And if she was still in distress, was there anything she or he could do about it?

Now that the interview was over, Verity's guard—McDonald, she had called him at one point—took the opportunity to kick him out.

"Okay, time to go."

Knox stood and watched Verity for a reaction.

She didn't meet his gaze but did stand and watch as his hands were bound again behind his back and his guards took up their posts around him again.

"Goodbye, Verity," he said on his way out.

"Goodbye," she answered, finally meeting his gaze.

He was led outside and back to his new living situation. And though it was another prison just by another name and with his mole Dr. Makzik, he was still happy to have seen Verity again.

16

VERITY

"HEY, ARE YOU OKAY?"

Verity turned and saw McDonald was staring at her, brows furrowed and a frown on his face.

How long had she been zoning out?

"About five minutes."

Shit. She'd said that out loud?

He handed her glass of water to her. She'd totally forgotten about it once Special Agent Kaur had arrived but she hadn't been able to focus on much once she'd seen Knox.

Now, they were both gone but she was still in a mental fog. It was less irritating than the frustration and low-level rage she had felt during and after her first meeting with the agent but she wasn't sure this was much better.

If she was dissociating again, she was getting worse—right?

And if she texted Dr. Hudson about her kidnapper being allowed into her house, she'd have to answer a lot of questions that she had no idea how to spin. She wasn't even sure about the REAL truth of how he'd gotten inside, and she doubted she ever would.

She took the glass of water from McDonald and forced

herself to take a sip even though it felt like her throat was almost completely closed with panic. She hadn't even felt this anxious as when she had been in the middle of fighting for her life and being kidnapped by aliens.

She swallowed and felt a wave of dizziness and nausea hit her. Before she could drop it, she placed the glass back down on the wooden dining room table—without a coaster, but she'd deal with the consequences later—and ran upstairs to her bathroom where she bent over the toilet again in what was now a familiar position.

The special alien treatment pills she'd been given—and she knew that for sure now even though Knox had refused to outright confirm it—were supposed to get rid of this symptom. Were they not working either? After a lot of deliberation, she had finally decided to continue taking them but maybe it had been pointless, after all. Though she doubted it. It was much more likely that this was a psychosomatic reaction to her anxiety at seeing Knox in her home.

She heard footsteps ascending the stairs and quickly stood up.

Was he back?

McDonald stood in the doorway. "You need anything?"

She shook her head.

He nodded and walked back down the hall to give her privacy.

Verity brushed her teeth and stared at her reflection.

She still hadn't seen any signs of iridescence on her skin after that one time but she also knew that she hadn't been dreaming that. Was it only a night thing? Or had it been some trick that Knox and his spies pulled on her to make her see him for answers?

She wasn't sure how they'd do that but she'd seen a few crime show episodes about the government could play some pretty messed up mind games with people. And if they could do it, she assumed the aliens could too. Probably better. She shuddered at the thought.

And that wasn't even taking into account how she'd felt about him touching her during the interview.

She should've felt disgusted, but she hadn't.

If anything, her body had welcomed it which only made her confused and angry at herself. Which probably explained the headache that had started forming right around that time before it had been subsumed by the mental fog she was still dealing with.

Would a steam shower make it go away?

Maybe she'd take a bath and get some of the tension out of her muscles and then take a nap so her body could relax.

As she'd expected, Special Agent Kaur had been incredibly nosy when it came to her and Knox's more personal interactions. But that didn't change how she'd cringed and tensed every time he voiced a question on the topic. Now she felt like a wind-up doll who was so close to cracking based on the amount of tension in her back and neck.

Decision made, she called out into the hall, "I'm taking a bath!" then shut the door before she could hear McDonald or Hughes confirm that they'd heard her. They'd have to be deaf not to have.

She turned on the faucet and pulled out her phone to check the time. Only four o'clock. Which meant the interrogation had only been an hour long instead of the eternity she had experienced.

Verity poured the last of the Epsom salts into the hot water and watched it dissolve immediately. She really needed to get more. Who knew that she'd be taking so many baths when she wasn't trying to get rid of soreness from dance? She texted her father's assistant for that and hit send. Then she turned a thirty-minute timer on and placed her phone on the sink. If she fell asleep this time, at least this would wake her up before anything bad could happen. One would think she'd wake up the moment she slipped under the surface but she'd woken up way too close to being submerged more than once and she didn't feel like accidentally drowning. It wouldn't be as bad as what happened to her on the ship but either one would lead to the same result, and she enjoyed living, thank you very much.

On a whim, she grabbed her last vanilla bath bomb and dropped that in, too. Then she stripped and got into the water, enjoying the immediate relief it provided as she sank deeper.

Thank goodness Knox's people hadn't tried to test her heat sensitivity by boiling her alive. That definitely would have permanently ruined baths and showers for her. She wasn't sure if it had ruined swimming yet, but at least in her own home, she could easily breathe and the only way she could drown would be if she fell asleep, or if someone attacked her. Though, the anxiety about being attacked in the shower had more to do with being stabbed like in *Psycho* than someone holding her under the spray.

She sighed and sank lower, submerging her shoulders. She really needed to stop thinking about all the ways someone could kill her. She'd drive herself crazy that way. Then Dr. Hudson's bill would *really* be through the roof. Though she supposed she was grateful her father was willing to pay for her at all.

Verity would text Dr. Hudson once she was done with her bath, but she could already feel the tension seeping back into her muscles. She took a deep breath and tried to release it again. She might as well get out of the tub now if she wasn't going to actually benefit from it but she didn't just waste her last vanilla bath bomb and her Epsom salts for a two-minute soak.

She shifted, feeling restless. Maybe she'd paint her nails and do a face mask to complete the "self-care" rituals that everyone always recommended online. She'd never done all of them at once before. Her father didn't really understand spa days, and neither had she but today felt like it called for it. If reuniting with your kidnapper and being forced to talk about it to a third party didn't qualify, did anyone ever "deserve" a self-care day?

She propped herself into a sitting position and closed her eyes. If she sank down a bit in her sleep, she'd be fine, and if she was lucky, she'd get some rest without having to wonder how fast time was passing.

The alarm finally went off and Verity opened her eyes, blinking away the fatigue that still lingered. She'd actually slept without any dreams. She had no idea when the last time that had happened. Verity couldn't believe it was the only time since her return, but she honestly couldn't remember the specific instance.

She'd never had a memory problem before but now she was having a problem remembering simple things about when things happened last. Another symptom of the changes happening to her? Or was it another awesome form of a trauma reaction? Because the internet had a never-ending list of those and if she was going to play bingo with the ones she had, she might win something. If it were free therapy, it would be relevant but not nearly rewarding enough for the suffering she was currently dealing with.

Verity sucked in a breath, bracing herself for the cold air, and stood up. She wrung her hair out and grabbed her towel off the rack. Then she stepped onto the fuzzy mat, letting it soak up the dripping water. Reaching over, she unplugged the bath and heard the tell-tale sound of it starting to drain.

As a kid, she used to always turn the water with her own hands, as if it wouldn't work without her creating whirlpools to help it along. Sometimes she still did it when she was impatient but she didn't care enough to do it this time. With her recent luck, watching the swirling water might make her nauseated all over again.

She needed to take another pill but she still wasn't happy at doing it when she knew it was exactly what Knox wanted her to do. Call it juvenile, but whenever it came to him, she wanted to do the exact opposite of what he said. She was also starting to feel that way about her father, which wasn't a great development, but he was also being unbearable. But aside from making her want to tear her hair out, Knox and her father were complete opposites who hated each other because of her kidnapping. If only they could put aside their issues to handle the invasion. Or, at the very least stop driving her nuts.

She sighed. She needed more women in her life. And while her doctors were helping, though she still had her suspicions about Dr. Lane, she wished her mom was alive right now to provide some much-needed perspective.

She cracked the door open and announced, "Coming out!" Looking both ways, she saw the hallway was empty and made a run for her room, shutting the door behind her. If someone had decided to ambush her there and then, she would've been screwed but luckily it was empty.

Verity dressed quickly, pulling on a loose set of sweatpants and a slightly oversized sweater. Normally, she liked form-fitting or even tight clothes but she didn't want anything constricting right now. She could still feel Knox's hand on her thigh like a brand. The bath had failed in getting rid of that body memory, but at least it had helped her relax.

She pulled up her phone and shot off a text to Dr. Hudson. Do you have time to talk?

Three dots appeared and then the reply came through. Does an hour from now work?

Verity sent a thumbs up and started pacing. She had the therapy session lined up but now she just had to figure out what to say.

17

KNOX

KNOX JOLTED UPWARD and felt a tug on his left arm. His eyes adjusted to the dark room and took in the needle and tube attached to his left forearm.

Dr. Makzik had inserted it while General Landau watched but the human hadn't known that the liquid being put into the bag was a modified version of his usual morning drink that he'd been missing since he'd landed on Earth. Dr. Makzik had explained it once they were alone but it essentially removed all the taste elements and was a pure energy shot for his bloodstream.

But he'd gotten pretty tired soon after, which she had explained was likely from the adrenaline crash of seeing Verity again. He wasn't sure that was it but she knew more about these details than he, so he wasn't going to question it.

He was alone in the medical room and the hallway was black but he could see his guards milling around as they passed back and forth in front of the doorway.

Knox leaned against the padded chair's headrest. It was much more comfortable than the metal one he'd been sitting on for days but he still would have liked the opportunity to lie down on the exam table instead to better distribute his mass since Earth's gravity was harder on Eochronians than humans. It's why his kind was generally taller than humans. They had altered the gravity on the ship for the humans on board but he assumed Eiz'm had set it back to normal once Knox had left—it's not as if his rival cared about making the humans comfortable.

He took a deep breath and focused on forgetting the latest dream he'd had of Verity. It hadn't been another sexy one like before but more of a loop of seeing her during their afternoon interrogation and the frustrating feeling of impotence at his inability to make her feel better.

He wasn't even certain what had woken him, but he could sense there was a reason to stay awake even though he couldn't find tangible proof for the gut feeling that something bad was about to happen.

Truly bad, not just an annoyance like being interrogated by General Landau late at night or any time by Special Agent Kaur.

Dr. Makzik poked her head in and said, "You're awake, Your Majesty?" quietly enough that the humans couldn't hear her deference to him.

He nodded.

She walked in and noted the bag feeding into him was empty. She unlocked a cabinet and pulled out another. After replacing it, she spoke again. "Do you need anything?" she asked louder. "Water? A blanket?" Thankfully, she didn't comment on his current aroused state.

"No, thank you, Dr. Lane," he said.

She nodded. "I'll be back to check on you later but if you need anything, don't hesitate to reach out."

He nodded and couldn't fight off the sleep already pulling him under again.

18

VERITY

VERITY WALKED through the dark halls of the medical building and resisted the urge to run. She'd been watching too many people play horror games that took place in abandoned hospitals and asylums. Hughes and McDonald had escorted her but she'd convinced them to stay in the waiting room since Knox was heavily guarded. She wasn't here for him, anyway.

She needed to find Dr. Lane and actually find out what had shown up on her blood tests, but the woman wasn't in her office. Maybe she was doing more tests on Knox right now? Only one way to find out.

She hadn't seen what room Knox had been assigned once she'd sprung him from the prison but there were only two directions to check, and the four guards posted outside his door were a dead giveaway. And even though she'd taken the alien treatment twice that day, they were surrounded by red outlines, allowing her to easily see them in the dark.

They all turned towards her in unison, almost as if they were androids with a hive mind. But she knew better. She'd seen enough drills that tested and trained their ability to act as a unit, even without verbal communication.

She walked closer and one from each side of the doorway moved to fill the gap before she could enter.

"No visitors allowed, Verity. Your dad's rule."

She rolled her eyes. Obviously it was his. Whose else would it be? Hell, if Special Agent Kaur were in charge, he'd probably want them together as much as possible to get more answers.

How could she get past them?

She remembered the guards in front of the prison building and how they had suddenly changed their tune when she had asked a second time while—was that it? Touching the back of her neck? It seemed silly but what was the harm in trying?

She rubbed the back of her neck again, as if she were nervous —which wasn't too much of an exaggeration—and asked again firmly, "Can I please see him?"

The guards looked at each other then let her pass.

What a weird superpower to have, but she wasn't about to complain. The question was did all Eochronians have it, and if so, why hadn't Knox ever used it on her? He had never touched his neck while talking to her in all the times they'd been together. But maybe there were other ways to trigger it that she didn't know?

That was a concern for another time.

She walked in and saw him sleeping.

And Dr. Lane cleaning his neck with an alcohol wipe and a syringe that had a suspicious blue liquid in its chamber lying on the nearby medical tray.

Verity stayed silent, waiting to see what happened next— hoping she was wrong—but when she saw the woman reach for the syringe, she moved forward. Acting on instinct, she ran inside and grabbed the woman from behind. She wrapped her arm around her middle and grabbed her wrist with the other hand as tightly as possible, pulling her away from Knox. A normal person would have dropped the syringe by now, only confirming her suspicion that Dr. Lane was in fact inhuman. But why was she turning on Knox?

The woman reached around and grabbed Verity's hair and yanked hard until she screamed.

The four guards ran inside and tried to pull them apart to detain the crazy doctor, but she threw them off one by one. Each one landed with a thump against a wall or a cabinet or the floor.

She heard them groan and saw they were all still breathing, but they weren't going to be much help. They were all out cold, which meant their heroic charge had been for nothing.

Then Verity got the same treatment as the STFs as the woman kicked her in the chest and her back slammed against the wall. She ducked before Dr. Lane threw a punch that broke the wall— right where her head had been a moment before.

But she wasn't done. Before she could escape, Dr. Lane grabbed Verity by her wrists, pinning them to her sides with enough pressure that Verity could feel them starting to crack.

Closing her eyes and hoping it would work, Verity brought her head forward hard and fast, hitting Dr. Lane in the forehead, sending her backward a few steps.

Verity heard footsteps running through the hall and saw the outlines of Hughes and McDonald run in.

McDonald ran to her while Hughes went after Dr. Lane.

She winced when the woman flipped him without a problem.

McDonald stood to protect her but was also quickly thrown to the floor.

While Dr. Lane's attention was diverted, Verity took the opportunity to tackle her to the floor but the woman grabbed her leg before she could reach Knox.

"Knox!" she cried out, hoping to wake him.

She didn't have time to see if she was successful before she felt Dr. Lane's arm wrapping around her neck, squeezing tight.

Verity gasped for breath and grabbed the woman's forearm,

trying to pull it away as she turned her head into the elbow like she'd been taught, but there was no leeway for her to move.

Even though it was already dark, Verity could tell her vision was starting to get spotty which meant she was running out of time. Was she going to die? Or was Dr. Lane only trying to incapacitate her? Surely she could have already snapped her neck but was instead choosing to cut off her oxygen.

Before she could sink into oblivion though, she heard the metal tray clatter as it collided into the wall, and then Dr. Lane was yanked away from her. Verity fell forward, barely catching herself on her hands before she face-planted into the floor.

She scrambled to her feet and turned to see Knox holding Dr. Lane in a headlock a moment before she heard a cracking sound.

Her jaw dropped open as she watched him ruthlessly snap her neck and drop her dead corpse at his feet.

Or, she assumed Dr. Lane was dead? Maybe Eochronians were like vampires and breaking their neck only temporarily incapacitated them? Maybe they needed to be beheaded or killed by piercing their heart with something special? And who knew if that something special even existed on her planet?

Knox's eyes landed on her and she stood frozen, unable to move. He'd just saved her life at the cost of one of his own kind.

Did that mean that she now owed him a debt? Would he demand she pay it? And in what currency?

Even in the dark, she could see him looking her up and down and his eyes flare with an intense heat, almost as if she were witnessing a brilliant supernova in his irises. She couldn't tell if it was anger or lust, but it was powerful enough to scare her all over again. She took a step backward, and he took one forward.

"Verity—" he started, his voice rough with sleep.

Before she could think about it again, she ran out of the room.

He could easily catch her, but she didn't hear him coming after her and she wouldn't make the stupid horror genre mistake of looking back. She was not about to trip over something only to be overpowered because of her own actions.

Verity took the stairs instead of the elevator. She had no idea if Knox would make it into the metal box with her before the doors closed, and she wasn't about to take the chance. She kept running until she got home and slammed the door shut.

Her father was standing there with his arms crossed and a glare darkening his features.

"Where—"

"Not now, Dad," she said sharply. "Dr. Lane was one of them. Knox just killed her to save me. She knocked his guards out when they tried to defend me after I attacked her. She was going to kill him in his sleep," she explained in a rush.

Her father's expression changed to one of deep skepticism but he no longer looked furious. "He saved you?"

She nodded. "He's free but I don't know if he stayed there or if he's on his way here or what. McDonald and Hughes were also knocked out, but I don't think any of the blows were fatal."

At least, she hoped not. She couldn't take any more losses of people protecting her.

"We'll have to discuss this tomorrow with Special Agent Kaur and our allies."

She nodded.

"But for now, go to bed and lock your door and windows."

"What are you going to do?"

"Handle the situation." He pulled out his phone and said something to one of the guards around the house. "Hughes and McDonald out of commission. Get me two more in the house and two more outside. The prisoner has escaped. Stay vigilant."

She could hear Flynn answer with a simple, "Yes, sir," before her father hung up.

He gave her a stern look. "You're still here?"

She dropped her gaze to the floor and ran upstairs, then paused to listen for any movement in her room.

Silence greeted her. Still paranoid, she tiptoed along the wall to her room and peeked in. No red outlines appeared but that didn't mean Knox wasn't there since he didn't seem to have one. No shimmering air either like the night she'd been taken or after she'd kissed Ben.

Thinking of him sent a punch of grief through her. She hadn't been able to think about him much with everything else happening but now she felt tears welling in her eyes again.

Verity entered her room, closed the door, and locked it as her father instructed. She walked to the window and tested that it was still locked, then quickly changed into sleep clothes and crawled under the covers.

She closed her eyes and felt the tears slide down her cheeks onto her pillow.

Ben had died protecting her. So had Harrison. She'd almost died protecting Knox, and he had saved her.

She knew being kidnapped by aliens would permanently complicate her life, but things were easier when she could think of Knox only as her captor with the frustrating ability to make her want him. Now that he'd actually taken care of her when he didn't have to? It was impossible to see him as a one-dimensional bad guy anymore. Which made her feelings towards him all the more confusing.

Dr. Hudson had reassured her that her reaction to seeing Knox again was understandable and nothing to be worried about but tonight's events only added another knot to her stomach when thinking about him.

She cursed and closed her eyes, praying sleep would come quickly and that everything would finally start resolving itself in the morning. The attack Knox had warned her about was still looming over the planet, but maybe her father would actually listen to him about how to defeat Eiz'm now that Knox had saved her—an action none of them could ignore.

19

KNOX

KNOX HEARD a groan and turned his head. Even from his horizontal position on the exam table, he could see his guards starting to get up from the ground.

Finding out Dr. Makzik had been the traitor, and likely the one framing him for Verity's guards' deaths, wasn't great but at least she was no longer a problem. And a bonus, he finally got to lie down comfortably. It's not as if the incapacitated guards could have prevented him from removing the needle in his arm and switching positions once Verity had left. And once they saw that he hadn't run away, maybe they would decide to leave it without him having to convince them.

One of his guards and one of Verity's were the first to recover. The others could almost be mistaken for corpses aside from the slight rising and falling of their chests indicating they were still breathing. Thankfully, Dr. Makzik hadn't gone on another killing spree. Even though he had killed her, he would still have been framed for mass murder—and that was already on top of Verity's two former guards.

The two humans walked over to him and then stared at each other, likely debating on what to do next.

Knox's guard started checking in on the others, nodding to his companion each time.

He saw Verity's guard touch his earpiece and whisper, "Flynn? Hughes here. McDonald is still out as are three of the prisoner's guards, but we're all alive. How is she?"

Knox heard the man on the other end say, "Home safe, sleeping now. General wants a meeting tomorrow with the prisoner. Do you need back-up?"

"A few would be great. I'm okay to keep going. So is Thomson," clearly referring to Knox's only conscious guard.

"Roger that."

A small click indicated the conversation was over.

Knox sat up and laced his fingers together in his lap.

Hughes and Thomson followed the action, and he held out his wrists. "Do you want to cuff me again?"

They exchanged another look.

Thomson grabbed a set of handcuffs from the small of his back and snapped them onto Knox.

He'd only suggested it because he didn't want to be taken back to the dungeon. His being restrained seemed to give them all some peace of mind though Trohm's escape and now Dr. Makzik's violent outburst was a clear reminder that it was a prop more than anything.

Knox heard more footsteps approaching and soon the room was completely filled with guards. Some watched him while others moved their fellow soldiers out of the way.

There were murmurings outside and he heard a discussion between the medical staff about where to put them and how to best take care of them in the other patient rooms.

He was certain no one was expecting so much activity tonight but he had to admit the humans were regrouping well. An emergency response strategy wasn't just about attacking the enemy and defending yourself, it was also taking care of those who DID inevitably get injured. Without that component, any injury became a death sentence regardless of scientific advancements that otherwise eliminated the unnecessary casualties.

Bored again, Knox lay back down and pulled up the star map. There was no change from what he'd seen the last time he checked. He contacted Trohm and didn't get an answer. He tried Zeph, and got a short automated message saying he was unavailable. His time on Earth had clearly affected him because no other Eochronian had a similar set up.

He doubted it would work but he tried Aerue again. When he was proven right, he was out of options aside from Dr. Mak'en, and he didn't feel comfortable asking her for information on Eiz'm so soon after murdering her sister. It had been in self-defense, of course—well, defense of Verity—but he doubted that would make the news any easier. And he didn't want to have a conversation with it hanging between them unsaid either.

Verity had accused him of lying to her before with lies of omission, and he had to admit she was right. He didn't want to do that with her anymore, and certainly not to Dr. Mak'en who had remained loyal to him amidst Eiz'm's coup even while her sister hadn't. At least, he thought she had. Then again, he'd been wrong about Dr. Makzik.

Again, he was in a room without any direct sunlight but he was luckily still energized enough from all the exposure he'd had while staying at Zeph's home. He'd stored some in his suit, too, but hadn't needed to dip into that reserve yet. Thankfully, the liquid Dr. Makzik had been pumping into his veins had only made him tired. At least, as far as he could tell.

Once he'd woken up, he'd been able to fight the traitor with the same speed and strength he usually had and he didn't have any dizziness or balance issues. Perhaps he hadn't received enough of a dose for it to be effective. Maybe his royal blood protected him whereas another of his kind would have succumbed. Or, if he was less lucky, the symptoms were insidious in its slow manifestation.

Knox pulled up his health monitor panel through his helmet and checked for evidence that something was wrong with him. His blood-oxygen levels were normal as were his cortisol levels, eliminating the only two reasons he could think of that could make him tired. Eochronians didn't follow the same circadian rhythm as humans so he doubted the mystery substance had targeted that part of his system. He doubted there was a way to trick a body into believing it had been without starlight for a human month since it wasn't a normal type of hallucination or even a psychosomatic symptom.

Whether he wanted to or not, he'd need to consult the medical team aboard his ship. Perhaps he'd contact Dr. Mak'en's assistant Brauhm instead. In truth, he was as intelligent as his boss but Knox had left it to Dr. Mak'en's discretion to promote the individuals on her team. Millenia had passed and she had yet to do it, though he had no idea why. Perhaps she was judging based on a set of criteria he was unaware of, or she was a control freak who would never give up more control than she already had by delegating to an assistant and team of other researchers.

He looked at the bag that still hung on the small metal hook attached to the thin, rolling stand. It wasn't the Eochronian clear truth liquid or the amber healing serum but a sapphire color he'd never seen before.

Knox was surprised none of the human guards who were now filling the room had noticed it. If they asked him, he honestly wouldn't be able to give them an answer as to its contents and the one person who could have was dead. He doubted a human scientist would be able to identify any of the chemical components of the liquid.

Knox opened a communication channel to Brauhm who thankfully answered immediately.

"How can I help you, Your Majesty?"

He typed out the message, I need you to study this, then activated the streaming capability of his helmet and looked at the medicine bag so Brauhm could see it. Knox zoomed in to see the individual molecules and their structure. It should be more than enough to get the scientist started. This put me to sleep. Don't tell Mak'en, he added.

Brauhm hesitated, a confused expression passing over his features, but he recovered quickly and nodded.

Knox ended the communication.

One of the guards shot him a suspicious look but Knox pretended to not see him out of his peripheral vision. To avoid any questions, he closed his eyes.

Though tonight had been unfortunate in ways he never could have anticipated, he suspected the crisis would earn him another meeting with Verity where they would be interviewed together to recount the incident. And he'd finally be able to clear his name of double murder by giving the name of the guilty party with the added reassurance she was now dead.

Unlike their afternoon conversation with Special Agent Kaur, they wouldn't merely provide different perspectives on the same event. He'd been so deeply asleep that he was also curious to hear her side to fill in the gaps. Him needing her to do so in the first place was disturbing. He had never been so out of his senses that he was completely unaware of his surroundings to the point of being vulnerable. And he had certainly been that when Verity had come in.

If it was anything like how Verity had felt the night Eiz'm had forcibly taken her from her bed, he now understood why she was so mad at him for issuing the order. It wasn't exactly the same though because it was his only crime against her while this had only been Eiz'm's latest offense. His original interactions with Verity had also been impersonal while Eiz'm's were always painfully personal as part of some vendetta against him.

Knox had never figured out why he hated him so much. It wasn't as if he had committed a crime against him, nor did he know any of his ancestors to have wronged Eiz'm's family that could potentially justify a blood feud. Nor had his father shown him any special preference that Knox had failed to continue, which would have understandably caused some resentment. He understood that some individuals instinctively hated each other. But for someone to go so far as to order an assassination attempt and ally with old enemies for a large-scale coup, he assumed there had to be a more specific motive.

Even Knox's frustratingly vehement dislike of Verity's human captain had stemmed from jealousy. It was an ugly reason but it was the truth. Knox had fought his personal attraction to Verity, but he wasn't so immature that he couldn't admit he had fallen victim to the overpowering emotion.

His mind drifted Verity. He wondered what she was doing now. The guard named Flynn had said she was safe, and he trusted that was the truth now that the traitor was gone. But he wouldn't be okay until he saw her again. For all he knew, Dr. Makzik could have planted something as the next step of a larger plan or as a back-up plan in the event of her death. Even the best scenario involved Verity being in pain after her fight with Dr. Makzik. He wished he'd been able to slip her some of the healing serum before she had run away from him. The listening devices that were in her home only gave him the sound of breathing so she seemed okay for now.

If he could take Verity away, he would be able to protect her with all his Eochronian technology, even if doing so would bring her closer to Eiz'm. But his rival had only targeted her because of what she meant to him. He didn't have a true motive to go after Verity, so as long as he kept them separate, he didn't see any issues. Trohm and Zeph would be able to protect her on board while he worked on freeing Aerue and reclaiming control.

Knox took a deep breath and forced himself to empty his mind until all he could think about was the back of his eyelids. Even though he could make a run for it and grab Verity, her not being fully healthy would make their escape more difficult and he didn't want to hurt her anymore—even if it was an unintentional side effect of his actions. Which meant he couldn't solve anything until the morning, when his guards would likely release him from the room for interrogation.

The proper time to escape would come soon, and when it did, he'd be ready.

20

VERITY

THE FOOTSTEPS WOKE HER. But they weren't directly outside her bedroom.

No, these were downstairs, but still sounded louder than they normally would without anyone stomping around. She could hear them speaking about last night as if they were talking directly to her instead of through her floor.

Her hearing had clearly improved again overnight.

Verity sat up and groaned. She'd felt a bit sore after her fight with Dr. Lane—though she was certain that wasn't her real name anymore—but that was nothing compared to what she now felt. It was as if all the muscles in her torso, front and back, had seized up. Even breathing hurt, though that could be from the woman actively injuring her ribs not just generalized pain. She had to imagine this is how accused witches felt when the proof of innocence test involved crushing individuals to death under a pile of heavy stones. Unsurprisingly, they had all died. And she had basically already experienced the drowning test, too.

If she weren't certain the Eochronians were more advanced than humans, she'd wonder if they were also superstitious about witches or something similar based on how they were treated her.

Verity heard someone climbing the stairs and jumped out of bed, hiding in the closet before there was a knock on her bedroom door and it cracked open. She hoped it was her father or one of her guards but whichever alien had entered their home to leave the note on her pillow—probably Dr. Lane since Knox had insisted it wasn't him—had proved their home was easy to infiltrate.

Whoever it was popped their head in, then opened it wider when they saw she wasn't in bed.

Looking through the slats in her closet door, she saw that it was her father, who looked like he was about to kill someone for allowing her to disappear.

She opened the closet door and he whirled around.

"Are you trying to give me a heart attack?" he shouted at her.

"I heard someone coming and thought this would be safer."

"You were already awake?"

Her waking up before he came to get her was a miracle on its own but that wasn't what she meant. "Yes, but I could hear everything happening downstairs. More than usual," she said, putting emphasis on the last words.

Understanding dawned on his face.

"How long?"

"Since last night?"

"Did Dr. Lane do anything to you?"

"Aside from kick my ass?"

He frowned.

"No," she answered.

"Are you still feeling sick?"

"I could use a horse tranquilizer right about now."

"Are you feeling up for a debrief today?"

She turned around and grabbed a sweater from her closet, pulling it on. "I don't think it can be avoided, Dad."

"I heard HE was in this house for your interview with Special Agent Kaur."

She nodded.

"Who let that happen?" His tone was sharp and promised retribution to whoever was responsible.

She shrugged. "To be fair, McDonald didn't leave me alone for a second with him."

Her father made a dissatisfied sound but didn't say anything else on the subject.

"Hughes watched him all night."

Verity felt a twinge of sympathy. That couldn't have been easy. Though Hughes' generally silent demeanor kind of reminded her of Aerue, now that she thought about it. Of course, that relationship lacked hatred between them so it wasn't exactly the same.

She was surprised Knox hadn't up and gone in the night, or tried to take her with him. Maybe his plans had changed? Though she wouldn't know either way since she still didn't know what his original one was.

"We'll go after you have breakfast," he said.

"I'm not hungry." She was in too much pain to even think about eating. "I promise I'll eat lunch later."

Before he could argue, she grabbed a pair of jeans from her cabinet and moved past him into the bathroom. She shut the door and quickly swapped pants before she started brushing her teeth with one hand hair with the other.

She met him downstairs where McDonald stood next to him.

"Let's get this over with," her father muttered.

McDonald checked in with Flynn who was in the security room and confirmed it was safe to exit. Then he left first.

Verity walked beside her father, forcing herself to slow down rather than moving at what now felt natural ever since her body had started changing. If she gave into her new instincts, she'd already be at the medical building and talking to Knox.

When they finally arrived, Verity walked in first and went through the security without a hitch. She waited for them to meet her at the elevator before they started the upward journey to her alien captor.

"Will Special Agent Kaur be joining us?" she asked, hoping the answer was no. She didn't feel like dealing with him when she was still hurting so much from a beat-down. She didn't need to give him any more ammunition for believing she wasn't a capable individual.

Her father shook her head, a small smile lifting the corner of his mouth.

The metal doors opened and she strode to the same room as the night before.

Verity heard Knox sit up before she even rounded the threshold. Knox sat on the examination table with his cuffed hands on his lap. He had laced his fingers together and appeared to be patiently waiting for her arrival.

Their gazes collided and the guards in the room, her father and McDonald at her back ceased to exist. As if pulled forward by an invisible string, she took a step forward. And then another until her knees were almost touching his.

This time, he was the one restrained but the situation reminded her of how aloof he'd been when they first met in his throne room. It had only been a month ago but it felt like a different lifetime.

Out of the corner of her eye, she saw Hughes reach for his weapon and heard McDonald do the same behind her.

A small smirk graced Knox's lips, letting her know that he found their protectiveness amusing, but he didn't do anything to provoke a more severe response.

Her father cleared his throat behind her and came into view, standing beside them.

"What happened here last night?" he demanded.

"Your daughter would know better than me," Knox answered. "I was indisposed for the start of the action."

He hadn't actually said anything annoying but she had the sudden urge to slap him.

Before she could take another step forward to do that, she felt a hand on her arm.

She turned and saw McDonald watching her with a forbidding expression that would have made Ben proud, and probably her father.

Verity shook off his grasp but took a step back from Knox to remove the temptation.

"What happened?" her father asked, turning his attention to her.

She faced him and forced herself to ignore the heat of Knox's stare on her as she answered. "I came here to talk to Dr. Lane about my blood tests, and she was about to inject him," she tilted her head toward the alien king, "with some blue liquid. I ran in to stop her."

"Why?" Knox asked.

Her father's lips pursed at the interruption but raised an imperious eyebrow at her, waiting for an answer.

She shrugged. She still wasn't totally sure why but her instincts had gone into overdrive and she hadn't taken the time to question herself at the time.

"And then what happened?"

"We started grappling, Hughes and the guards outside came in to help me but Dr. Lane—" she cut herself off and waited for Knox to fill in her real name.

"Makzik," he supplied.

"Makzik attacked them and they went down like they were bowling pins."

She heard Hughes grunt in offense but he couldn't argue with her telling of events.

"And then she went back to fighting you?" her father asked.

"Was about to kill me when Knox saved me."

"Were you waiting for that?" her father asked.

"Dad! He saved my life."

"I know that. But the timing is a little suspicious."

"Dad—"

"You have to consider it," he continued. "He could have protected you from his own mole if he really cared about your safety. Instead, he saves your life to get on my good side when he could have easily intervened sooner."

She hadn't thought Knox was slouching but now that he straightened at the thinly-veiled accusation reminded her of how tall he really was.

"I had nothing to do with your daughter's endangerment."

She turned and raised an eyebrow at him.

"Last night," he amended, having the grace to look chastised. "And I've never intentionally put her in harm's way."

"Forgive me if I don't believe you," her father grumbled.

"Your daughter has said the same thing," Knox said.

She and her father briefly made eye contact before both glaring at Knox.

He ignored her father and flashed her an unabashed smile instead.

She fought the smile trying to make its way onto her face. Stupid mirror neurons. Because there was nothing to genuinely smile about. At least, not for her. He seemed stupidly pleased about something, though she wasn't sure what that was.

Verity's father crossed his arms and took a step closer to Knox. "Why were you indisposed?"

"Dr. Makzik injected me with a sedative."

"What kind?"

Verity rolled her eyes. There was no way Knox was going to answer that. But she had another question pop into her mind. "She was really a doctor?"

He nodded.

"How did it put you to sleep?" her father interjected.

"I have no idea," the alien responded. "I've never seen it before."

"But it's still Eochronian?" she asked.

He looked impressed that she remembered the name of his kind. "Undoubtedly," he said. "The molecular breakdown isn't akin to anything on Earth."

"How do you know that?" her father asked.

Knox merely cocked his head towards him before redirecting his attention back to her.

She fought the urge to shift on her feet.

As if sensing her discomfort, McDonald grabbed the rolling doctor's chair from the corner of the room.

Verity sat down gratefully and crossed her legs. She didn't miss the way Knox's gaze followed the movement.

From her father's deep grunt, he didn't miss it either.

"You said there was an impending attack. Was she a part of it?"

Knox finally tore his eyes away from her and turned to fully face her father, crossing his legs on the padded table. "My rival is spearheading the violent attack against Earth. Given she clearly betrayed me, it had to be for him, so I would say yes. But as I established earlier, she was a doctor. Not a soldier. Even Eiz'm wouldn't utilize her for something she is unqualified for."

"And you have no other information?"

"He said the jerk has teamed up with their old enemies who are bigger fighters." She held her father's gaze to make sure he understood the implications.

He glanced away and she knew that he had finally come to the same conclusion as her. They needed Knox, whether they liked it or not.

21

KNOX

KNOX GLANCED around the living room and smiled at its homey appearance. He hadn't seen it for himself during his last visit to the Landau house but it was interesting to see the different decor style to Verity's room, the utilitarian kitchen, and old-fashioned dining room.

This space was somehow softer than the others, not just due to the presence of more pillows and materials other than leather and hardwood finishes. If he had to guess, Verity's mother had designed the room and neither Verity nor her father had changed it since she passed away.

He wondered if it was a conscious decision on their part to preserve this kind of shrine or if neither were aware of what they had done, and simply didn't want to rock the boat. The two surviving Landau's were so similar he could see them keeping the status quo merely by never having the conversation with each other.

If he ever brought it up, Verity would probably deck him. He smiled, almost wishing it would happen. But he didn't need her mad at him again. They'd be throwing punches at each other soon enough. For fight training, of course, but it would finally give her the opportunity to act out her frustration with him. He'd seen her pull herself back from smacking him more than once, and he was sure she would take full advantage of this excuse.

"This is a bad idea," the guard named Hughes said, checking the foyer again even though it was just as empty as the last time he'd glanced over his shoulder.

The human needn't worry. Knox would hear the General arriving long before he appeared anyway.

"You keep saying that," the other guard said. Verity had called him McDonald.

"You're saying you don't agree?"

"Of course I do. I didn't like him being here to talk to Special Agent Kaur either but everything went fine then."

Did that mean the man trusted him?

"I think what you mean to say is it didn't go wrong."

McDonald shrugged.

Knox looked at Verity who had remained silent during this exchange.

She sat in the gray armchair between the men, looking both bored and simultaneously amused at her guards' bickering. Not in a manipulative way but like an older sibling might find the younger's antics entertaining.

Knox had certainly seen that expression on Aerue's face more than once regarding Arfilmea's actions. Though he doubted he found any humor in her aligning herself with Eiz'm.

If he was going to justify the guards' concern, he already would have spirited Verity away from here. The fact that he hadn't should have gained him more of their trust but that hadn't yet happened. He was starting to doubt it ever would.

Now that he'd decided to stay longer, it made sense to have the support—as begrudging as it may be—of the humans. All his few remaining Earth-bound allies were scattered across the world, his best agents were back on the mothership, and he had learned he wasn't as invincible as he'd thought.

"Guys," she finally spoke up. "He's standing right there, and can hear everything you're saying. Besides, if you didn't think it was a good idea, you didn't have to open the door for him."

"He would have broken it anyway," Hughes said.

"I would not have," Knox objected. He wasn't an animal. He would have merely disabled the lock and opened the door like a civilized being.

Verity slanted a look at him but then spoke to her guard instead. "Whatever. My point is, debating whether his presence is a danger is something you two should have discussed before now. It's moot at this point. Besides, he said he's going to teach us how to fight aliens."

"Do you really believe he's going to teach us how to kill them?" McDonald asked, crossing his arms and shooting a glare at Knox. "He knows we'd use that knowledge against him at the first chance."

"He promised to teach us to fight. He never said anything about teaching us to kill them," Verity said.

She wasn't outright defending him but it felt like she was on his side in the conversation all the same. Was she softening up to him? Or was that only her logical tactician side speaking?

She stood up and met his gaze. Fire sparked in her hazel eyes, making them temporarily appear more amber than their normal greenish gray. "Let's do this thing already."

"You already know how to fight," he said.

"Then why are we doing this exercise?"

"You didn't let me finish. You already know how to fight, but even though you held your own against my guards on your way off my ship—"

"I wouldn't have stood a chance if you hadn't commanded them to let me through."

She didn't sound happy about it but he was relieved that he wasn't going to be the one to break the news to her.

Her pride had flared more than a few times during their short acquaintance on his ship, and he didn't want to be on the target end of it right now when he was trying to help her.

"You've gotten faster and stronger than you used to be."

She nodded in confirmation.

"But you can't fight those new and improved instincts," he continued. "You're never going to stand a chance against an Echronian or a Vruxol if you're holding back."

"That's it?"

"No." He moved behind her slowly and she flinched, turning to face him again. They were close enough that her chest brushed his but neither of them bridged the small distance to bring their bodies flush against each other.

He ignored the disapproving sounds that emitted from her guards and focused on the task at hand.

"What are you doing?" she demanded.

"I'm going to teach you how to kill one of my kind." It was true that he hadn't promised to earlier but he wanted her safe, and that meant being able to kill Eiz'm or any of his traitorous supporters if he wasn't there to protect her.

She turned her head, almost looking over her shoulder at him but not quite. "Is that wise?"

"You need to know how to defend yourself against Eiz'm."

"How do you know I won't go after you?"

He knew the question was probably meant to be more biting but it came out in a more breathy tone which made lust start to curl in his abdomen.

He took the small step forward until they were touching everywhere and enjoyed the way she gasped.

"Because you need me on your side." He slid his hand down her side and pressed a spot right underneath her ribcage. "If you stab upward towards the heart in the center... you'll kill us."

"With anything?"

"A weapon would be helpful."

She huffed out a laugh. "Is that the only way to kill your kind?"

"Our armor is impervious to your bullets."

"Then how am I supposed to stab through it?"

"You're not a normal human. If you use your full strength, you could pierce it."

"Isn't that a design flaw?"

"Our kind has been united for as long as I can remember. An insurrection wasn't a consideration when our technology was being constructed."

She turned around and took a small step back. He saw her shake off her desire and square her shoulders. "What about a headshot?"

"Armor, again."

"Even if I ran at you?"

"My kind, you mean?"

She refused to confirm his correction and raised an eyebrow, demanding an answer.

"You probably could, but I think going for the heart would be a better bet. If someone sees you going for the head, they have more opportunities to block you."

"And these rules apply to Eochronians and Vruxols?"

"More or less."

"That's not helpful."

"Vruxol's have stronger, armor-like skin. But because of that, they're more arrogant and leave more gaps open in their armor. The throat is a vulnerable target but it won't kill them. It takes a long time for either of our species to bleed out, and we both have superior healing abilities compared to humans."

"Awesome." The sarcasm dripping from the single word made it clear just how happy she was with the situation.

"Okay," he said. "Come at me."

"Don't have to ask me twice."

She took one, large step back then ran at him and he prepared himself to counter, reveling in finally living the fantasy of getting to see her unleashed and matching their fighting skills.

22

VERITY

THE FRONT DOOR OPENED, and Verity glanced over her shoulder to see her father enter the house.

She heard McDonald grunt and a thud as Knox laid him out right before she felt the air rush towards her as he came at her.

He moved so fast that she barely had time to move out of the way but she managed it.

For a moment.

Then he grabbed her waist by twisting his arm as he passed her. It was a move that she'd done countless times in dance class, but her partner's intention was never to bring her down or injure her.

If anything, it was always a fancy lift that normally turned into a flip or her going up en pointe with an arabesque as her partner helped her rotate.

Knox did have the decency to cushion her fall by keeping his arm there as she fell to the ground, but it didn't do much for her comfort.

"What is happening here?" her father roared. He was angrier than she'd ever heard him, even when he was barking orders at the STFs after a particularly bad training day.

She sat up and accepted Knox's proffered hand. He pulled her up and she faced her father.

"Knox is teaching us how to fight his kind."

"And that involves roughhousing you?"

She rolled her eyes. This was the man who insisted she study alongside his STFs and ordered the instructors to not take it easy on her even though she was a civilian?

"It's fine, Dad."

"Her fighting technique is very good," Knox said, speaking up beside her.

Her father didn't spare him a glance but walked into the living room and deposited himself in the armchair they'd moved to the side to make more room for their practice.

He reached into his pants pocket and clearly hit the remote to Knox's shock collar based on Knox's stiffening and grimace.

Should they continue when she could feel his disapproval emanating so strongly it practically choked the air? She exchanged a look with McDonald who had gotten to his feet during her conversation. Knox hadn't offered to help him up like he had for her.

He gave a slight shake of the head.

Verity walked into the kitchen. He and Knox followed her. She heard her father's heavy footsteps, too. She gave them both glasses of water again and took one for herself. Then she grabbed a bottle of beer for her father and handed it to him.

He took it but didn't drink. Probably didn't want alcohol to affect his functioning while Knox was nearby.

She took a long sip of her water and caught Knox watching her again. She swallowed and placed the half-full glass in the sink. She'd handle it later. "Now what?" she asked the men.

No one answered.

"Where's he going to stay?" she asked, voicing the question no one had the guts to mention before. "Here?"

"Over my dead body."

She glared at her father. They had come way too close to that being a reality the night she was abducted.

"He can't stay in the medical center." Dr. Makzik might be dead but that didn't mean it was safe for Knox there. She might have others pretending to be humans just as Knox had Trohm hidden amongst the STFs.

"Where do you think he should stay?" he challenged.

"Somewhere where we can keep an eye on him," she answered without hesitation.

Her father crossed his arms. "And is there a reason you didn't think the cell would be a good alternative to the medical center?"

She glanced at Knox who seemed amused by the whole conversation.

"Because we all know that he could break out of there before we even finished chaining him back up," she answered. "Trohm did."

Her father huffed. "He can stay chained up in the basement."

Okay, now her father sounded a bit like a serial killer. It also made her think of more than a few werewolf shows where the supernatural creatures did that to stop themselves from hurting others. But Knox wasn't an animal overcome by violent impulses. At least, she didn't think so. And he'd already chosen to stay much longer than she expected him to.

"If he wanted to hurt me, he would have already," she said.

Her father started to argue but Knox cut in.

"She's telling the truth, General. And I would never hurt her. I explicitly gave my people orders to not harm her."

"And they didn't listen?" Her father sounded as skeptical as she had when she first met the alien king.

"Obviously not," she cut in, earning a glare from her dad. "What?" she asked. "I'm just pointing out the obvious. Otherwise, we wouldn't be worrying about an alien invasion right now."

"If you believe him," McDonald said, speaking up for the first time since her father had arrived home.

Verity threw her hands up. "What would you do, then?"

No one said anything, and she huffed indignantly. "That's what I thought."

She brushed past them, forcing herself to ignore the way her skin ignited with heat when her shoulder brushed Knox's because the infuriating alien refused to move out of her way.

Verity ran upstairs to her room and slammed the door shut. She belly-flopped onto her bed and screamed into her pillow in frustration.

Why were they being so stupidly stubborn?

Invisibility wasn't a new power she'd acquired from her alien transformation but she might as well be from a decision-making perspective. When would people start listening to her point of view?

She flipped over and stared out her window.

Far away, Eiz'm was plotting some genocidal campaign against humanity. They didn't have any more time to be squabbling over insignificant and moot details about Knox's ability to escape.

They needed to be a united front, or they'd never stand a chance. In short, they were most likely fucked.

She let out another scream, this time, not bothering to muffle herself. Let them hear her. Maybe they'd finally pull their heads out of their asses and make some peace with each other.

But she wasn't about to hold her breath.

Verity took a deep breath. Feeling more level-headed, she went back downstairs to tell the guys exactly what she thought. She was sick of them not listening to her, and she wasn't going to let any of them—or anyone else—die due to their stubbornness.

AFTER AN HOUR-LONG NAP Verity didn't remember falling asleep for, she went back downstairs and found the men sitting in tense silence around the dining room table. Hughes had joined her father, Knox, and McDonald at some point.

No dinnerware was set before them which made their location strange. Especially since they all could have kept their distance from each other better in the living room.

The only open chair was between her father at the head and Knox on one of the longer sides of the table. The other head of the table had lacked a chair ever since her mother had died, but she really would have liked one now.

Just her luck. She didn't feel like playing Switzerland when she was still mad at both of them.

Their gazes lifted from the wooden table to her, demanding she take her place between them.

Instead, she passed behind Hughes and McDonald, avoiding her father and Knox as much as possible, and walked into the kitchen where she grabbed a bottle of ginger beer and reached for her father's best rum from the liquor cabinet.

He never really touched it except when he was entertaining other top brass of the country's military. Very boys' club to the point that it was as if they had taken a time machine to an even more patriarchal time.

But she needed a strong drink if she was going to deal with him and Knox. And he couldn't ground her—for want of a better —any more than he already had. Besides, she'd been of legal age for four years and rarely drank to begin with. She deserved this small indulgence.

Verity poured a generous amount of each liquid into a cocktail shaker she pulled from the same cabinet and started mixing them until it sounded like she was playing the maracas.

She glanced over her shoulder, half-expecting someone to be watching her but she was alone. She continued and finally poured the mixture into an old-fashioned glass.

She put the bottles back, rinsed the shaker and put it in the dishwasher, and then walked back to the dining room.

She took a sip as she sat down, ignoring the disapproving stare her father sent her.

Knox turned toward her and eyed the glass in her hand. If she were on an actual date where her partner was having dinner with her and her father to meet the parents, she would have asked if he wanted something. But that dream scenario was so far from reality that she had no qualms about being selfish in her forgoing a hostess' normal offer.

McDonald shot her a sympathetic glance and looked as if he wanted a sip. Hughes had a similar expression. But they'd never ask, and she wouldn't give it to them while they were on duty. They all knew it would be irresponsible of them to drink while on the job, so it was better to leave the pointless conversation unspoken.

"What are you drinking?" Hughes asked.

"Dark and stormy," she said.

He nodded, clearly approving of her taste in alcohol.

He had been at her twenty-first birthday bash with the other STFs but they hadn't seen each other much that night. He'd been on the other side of the bar for most of the night, chatting with a few girls who had found his strong, silent demeanor attractive.

Verity couldn't remember if he'd actually taken any of them home that night.

She took another sip and ignored Knox watching her mouth on the rim. But just to screw with him a little, she licked her lips despite there not being any spare drops of liquid. She felt his legs shift next to hers under the table and smiled into her glass.

Verity drank small sips in silence until she finished it. She pushed the glass toward the center of the table and laced her fingers together in front of her.

She finally turned to Knox. "Any idea about why I'm reacting the way I am to whatever science experiment your people have done on me?"

He grimaced, and she thought it was at her question until she saw her father move out of the corner of her eye. "Will you stop with the collar, dad?" she snapped.

He didn't answer but Knox relaxed in his seat next to her.

He cleared his throat. "I suspect it's because your female and your hormones are heightening and perhaps accelerating your symptoms."

She sighed. Great. Just another reason to hate being female. Periods, patriarchy, and now pain caused by alien science.

He looked apologetic, as if he could tell the direction her thoughts had taken.

"And there's nothing you can do to stop them?"

"The medicine—"

"That your traitor gave me? You really think I'm going to take it after she tried to kill both of us?"

"It's the same treatment as you received on the ship. If you felt better while taking it, then part of your discomfort—"

"That's putting it mildly—"

"Is likely due to withdrawal after you abruptly stopped receiving it regularly on my ship."

Verity felt her father tense in his seat and placed her hand on his leg before he could reach for the shock remote again.

"It was in the food?"

Knox nodded.

She knew it!

Verity leaned back in her seat and stewed. The alien king had really only confirmed her suspicions but it didn't lead to any solutions for her personal situation or how to get the whole planet and all of humanity on board to fight Eiz'm and his army.

23

KNOX

THE GENERAL SUDDENLY PUSHED BACK FROM the table and stood. Everyone else did the same, and he was the last to rise, unsure if this was common etiquette due to the man's rank or if it was because this was his home. If Trohm were still here, he could have asked him.

"I need to debrief the other leaders," the man declared before walking out of the dining room towards the front door.

Verity and her guards followed.

Knox did, too, unsure of whether he was supposed to or not.

She shot him a look over her shoulder, and motioned him to walk with her. The five of them left the house and started walking towards one of the base buildings he'd never been in before. It was in the opposite direction of where he'd been kept and not super close to the medical center, either.

Verity gave him another look, this one much more mischievous than the last. Then, without any further warning, she took off at full speed, running to their destination. Her long, blonde hair, which was normally pulled back, flared out behind her like a golden train.

He started running, pursuing her even though he could easily overtake her as a pure-blooded Eochronian. But he didn't know where they were specifically going, and this was much more fun.

Knox heard her laughing and felt a ball of warmth bloom in his chest at the sound. He liked her happy. Hopefully, once Eiz'm was dealt with, he'd hear her laugh and see her smile much more frequently.

She came to a halt in front of a three-story brick building with glass and metal doors.

Not exactly secure, but since he assumed this was an office building on the most secure military base in the country, he assumed the humans hadn't worried about it being an issue prior to his kind's invasion four weeks ago.

She turned around and stared into the distance, waiting for her father and guards to reach them but he kept watching her until she finally looked at him.

"That was fun," he said.

She nodded, pushing some strands out of her eyes.

He wished he'd done it first. It would have given him an opportunity to touch her again.

"You were holding back though."

It wasn't a question from her.

Now, it was his turn to nod.

"Weren't you just lecturing me on the importance of not doing that?"

"In a fight," he clarified. "Besides, I had to follow you for directions."

"Are you sure it wasn't because you didn't want to admire me from behind?"

He smiled. "That might have been part of it."

She rolled her eyes and gave into the smile threatening to lift her luscious lips.

"You are such a guy," she said. "Alien king or not."

"Is that a bad thing?"

She shrugged, though he could see her pulse beating rapidly

at the base of her neck. Was it still from their burst of exercise or because of him? He hoped it was the latter.

And his thoughts weren't without some merit. Like him, she wasn't out of breath from the exertion, which made him believe her body was almost as fit as his now. Though probably less durable due to her human DNA. He wouldn't want her having to take a bullet even while wearing Eochronian armor. It would still protect her from a fatal wound but he bet she would be bruised and injured from the impact that he never would be.

They stared at each other in silence until the others caught up, all wearing matching thunderous expressions.

Before any of them could utter a word, Verity pushed the door open and went inside. He followed her and watched her walk through a plastic archway with lights on the top and a gray pad of some sort on the ground with the outlines of feet printed onto it.

The light turned green and he did the same but was stopped by the uniformed men on the other side who patted him down very thoroughly.

He saw the smirk on Verity's face and winked at her, setting off a blush that colored her cheeks with a luminous pink.

Finding nothing, the guards let him through and they waited only a few moments as the general and Verity's protection detail also passed through the machine.

"What is that?" he asked as they walked towards some metal doors and a metal panel with buttons on it.

"A metal detector," she answered without looking at him. She pushed the button on top and he watched as a halo lit around the metal circle. "But I'm going to guess none of your technology is made from Earth metals."

"Correct," he said.

The doors opened and she walked in first. Before he could, the guard named McDonald pushed past him followed by Hughes. He slid inside before the general could do the same.

Verity glanced at her father, then selected a number from the internal button panel.

She lifted her chin to watch a panel near the ceiling with carved out numbers, and he watched as each one was illuminated in turn until they reached the top. There weren't many as the building wasn't tall, but it was still better than trying to observe Verity while three men who hated him were glaring at him.

The doors opened again and he followed on her heels before they could be separated again.

A woman behind the desk stood up, an alarmed expression on her face upon seeing him. "Sir, I'm sorry, you can't go back there."

He kept walking and saw her glance over his shoulder, and she sat back down.

Whatever the general had indicated, clearly he had been deemed safe enough to enter the offices behind the door Verity had disappeared behind.

She was no longer in his sight but he heard her footsteps loudly enough that she could have been walking in heels on a hard wood surface rather than sneakers on carpet.

He found her sitting at a wooden table in a spacious, corner office. She tapped her fingers in a mesmerizing rhythm.

He took the seat beside her and waited for the human men to join them once again.

If he had still intended to take Verity, he would have done so while they were running to the building but they still looked at him as if he were about to steal their pride and joy the moment they let their guard down.

The general was the last one to enter and slammed the door behind him. He strode to his desk in front of the large window, his muscles taught with tension, and reached underneath.

Knox heard locks engage and inwardly sighed. Another prison. At least he wasn't alone this time.

The guards sat down in less fancy chairs flanking the door and staring directly at him.

The general clicked a few things on his computer and a screen on the opposite wall lit up. One by one, rectangles featuring different uniformed individuals populated the screen until twenty filled it. Various skin colors and medals distinguished them from each other, though Knox had no idea who any of them were.

A severe-looking woman spoke first. "What's the emergency, Landau? It's my granddaughter's first birthday party today."

"I'm sorry to hear that, Grand Marshal Yi, but this is important. There's an impending and likely imminent extraterrestrial attack."

She sat up straighter, bringing herself closer to the screen, her eyes taking in the general, Verity, and finally Knox.

"And how do you know this?"

Verity's father pointed at him. "He's their leader."

"Then why isn't he imprisoned?"

"Because he didn't order the attack," Verity said sharply.

A man on screen cleared his throat. "No disrespect, young lady, but—"

"My daughter is a vital witness to what these aliens are capable of," the general cut in. "If we want to have any chance of beating them, we need to listen to her."

The man on screen swallowed his protest but still seemed displeased about talking to people other than military officials.

Knox glared at him, and if Eochronians were gifted with the ability to incinerate people through eye contact alone, the man would be dead—ignoring the fact that they were separated by miles and digital screens. But how dare the man disrespect a general's daughter?

Verity had made it very clear that her country didn't have royalty when they met—a fact he was well aware of before she'd shared it—but it was still custom to defer to people based in part on their lineage on this planet.

In some ways, it offended him more on her behalf than the

special agent's annoyingly sexist and condescending attitude toward her.

Another woman on screen spoke, breaking the tension. "Tell us more about this invasion..." she trailed off as she looked at him.

"Knox," he said before flicking his wrist, pulling up his star map. He didn't want anyone knowing how to operate his armor, even if it was invisible to them. He adjusted it to the human light spectrum by surreptitiously tapping his ring finger and thumb together a few times. He suspected if he kept it ultraviolet, no one else but Verity would see it. And he didn't want to freak her out about her abilities again.

Their earlier race was the first time she seemed to have fun with them and didn't only consider them a reminder of her time as a scientific experiment for both her father and him. He pushed the comparison out of his head and cleared his throat.

"The largest ship is my own, currently parked near Jupiter." He ignored the surprised gasps. "The smaller ones are enemy Vruxol ships. My kind are stronger, faster, and harder to kill than humans. They are larger and stronger than my kind."

He watched the adorned individuals shift uncomfortably in their seats. Even though he could only see them from the waist up, it was clear his words disturbed them.

"How soon will they be here?" The same woman asked.

"It could be hours," he said, hearing the general start in his chair behind his desk. "It's only a matter of time. The only reason Eiz'm has taken so long to attack Earth is that he first had to subdue my supporters."

He met Verity's gaze and saw understanding in her gaze.

"Eiz'm?" someone asked the same time that someone else asked, "Subdue?"

He turned back to the screen.

"Eiz'm is a member of my army who has staged a coup in my

absence. I'm the king," he added in response to some of their blank expressions.

"Then why are you on Earth alone?"

He felt Verity's leg start bouncing under the table like it had the day before and yet again, reached for her. And just like last time, she stopped immediately but didn't push his hand away from her thigh.

Knox merely smiled and refused to answer the question. He wasn't alone but he wasn't going to reveal that small detail. The people physically in the room with him already knew that he hadn't been, and while it was true he was now alone on the base, he wasn't alone on the planet. Moreover, he hadn't told Verity his true plan of being there–though she was smart enough to have guessed his intentions—so there was no chance he was going to tell anyone else in the room or on the virtual call.

"Should we be expecting any other alien species?" Verity's father asked gruffly.

"No," Knox answered. "The Lielneh won't concern themselves with matters that don't directly affect them. We are all lucky they aren't aligning with my enemy." He took a deep breath and acknowledged the unfortunate truth. "They're smarter than my kind, which means humanity would be doomed from the outset."

He could feel all the humans around him bristling except one. Verity didn't seem offended like her father or the others, though he had expected her pride to make an appearance. Instead, she seemed pensive. But she wasn't trembling with fear, either, which he took as a good sign that she was still feeling okay.

If she ever became truly terrified, then he would know something was terribly wrong.

Then again, none of this was new information to her since he'd already told her when she'd visited him in his cell.

"So," the woman who'd asked him about the threat said. "What can we do?"

"What we already planned to," Verity's father answered. "The coordinated strategy we've spent years working on."

"I think you should be more specific, Dad," Verity interjected.

Knox watched the man turn his attention to his daughter in surprise.

"I'm just saying," she continued, "that maybe you should lay out the plan of attack for Knox so he can point out any deficiencies. It is his area of expertise."

"I'm not risking our planet's military playbook," he said then addressed the guards. "Please escort my daughter home and him back to lock up in the cell."

They approached him and put his cuffs on again. In front of him so it wasn't quite as bad as when they'd first "captured" him. Ever since he had saved Verity last night, the guards had seemed to trust him marginally more and this was the only way they showed it. They were never going to speak out against the general but his shoulders were glad for their small rebellion.

Still, Knox sighed. It seemed his prison break wasn't meant to last, after all. At least he hadn't gotten shocked too many times by the collar. He wished for its removal but none of the human men made a move to relieve him of the device.

Very well. He could live with that.

"I'm going with him," Verity announced, walking out of the room before her father could stop her.

Knox followed while flanked by her guards and the four of them walked through the hall back to where they'd come from.

As they descended, Knox noticed the guards looking and each other in silent communication. Though no words were spoken, he was positive it was about what to do about Verity's proclamation and probably whether it was worth invoking her father's wrath by letting her spend more time with him.

The doors opened and they quickly walked to the building's entrance.

This time, he saw Verity preparing to run before she did, and he took off before her, knowing exactly where they were going this time.

He heard the guard shout and issuing orders into their microphones even as he ran beside Verity—she'd caught up to him easily, which was a pleasant surprise.

The men were probably worried he making an escape attempt, though he wondered how they were justifying the part where he hadn't grabbed Verity to take her with him. She had followed HIM.

Together, they ran through the base, into the building, and down the stairs to his cell. They slowed down to a human pace and he opened the hidden door for her, daring her to follow him to the other side of the glass.

She stared up at him with a defiant expression and accepted the challenge as she not only joined him but moved around him until she was leading the way.

She paused in front of the last door that would bring them into the cell and stared at the key pad.

"May I?" he asked.

She shook her head and instead continued her inspection of it before typing in the code he would have based on the residual heat signatures even though it was from two days ago.

He wouldn't have been able to see that without his armor. The fact that she could while not being a pure Eochronian was a little unsettling. Everyone, including him, had assumed that the hybrid status would weaken any enhanced abilities she might develop.

It hadn't occurred to him that she could somehow be superior. Was it an instance of producing a grander result than merely adding together individual components? Didn't humans had a saying about that very phenomenon?

She walked around the chair, running her finger over the edges.

He felt arousal start to stir inside him again, imagining her doing the same to his body.

She picked up the chains that had been left there and lifted an eyebrow at him.

He took them from her and winked. "Let's save that for later."

She blushed. "Don't count on it."

"Then why did you follow me in here?"

"Curiosity."

The guards finally arrived and rushed forward upon seeing them together.

Verity turned toward them and raised her hand in a stopping motion to halt their panicked motions.

She walked to the door, and Knox didn't stop her.

"Will I see you again?" he asked.

She met his gaze over her shoulder. "Yes."

Then she was gone. She didn't bother to watch the guards were chaining him up again and instead walked away from him without another backward glance.

24

VERITY

THE NEXT MORNING, Verity and her father went to visit Knox again. For the first time, her dad hadn't argued about her being able to see him.

Maybe he was finally trusting her instincts, or at the very least had partially acknowledged that Knox was only forthcoming in her presence. Though, *forthcoming* was maybe an overstatement when the alternative is the complete silence she saw in the recordings of him.

At the door to the stairway, Verity could hear the chains rattling with her enhanced senses. By the time they entered the fluorescently lit space, Knox was already awake and waiting for them with a knowing smile on his face.

"You're still here," her father said, stating the obvious.

Knox tilted his head at them as if trying to see through them. "Did you expect different? We all know I could have escaped long before now. The chains are unnecessary. I'm staying to help you."

"Help yourself, you mean," her father snapped.

Knox didn't argue so Verity assumed her dad was partially right.

"There's something I still don't understand," Verity spoke up.

Both men turned to her, waiting for her to continue.

"Why are people going along with Eiz'm? Doesn't everyone know he's an asshole?"

"He does have an army behind him."

"So do you. Are you telling me no one stood up to him or thought to just take him out?"

Knox shrugged as much as the chains allowed. "I haven't been able to reach my agents on board."

"Are you sure they're on your side? I mean, Dr. Makzik had you and my dad fooled."

"But not you?" her former captor asked.

"I had my suspicions."

"Why didn't you tell me?" her father demanded.

"I wasn't sure you'd believe me, and I didn't have any proof."

"What made you suspicious?" Knox asked.

"Something about the way she was moving around you while she was last here alone with you."

Even so far away, her improved vision let her see the impressed flash of pride in his galaxy eyes.

"To answer your inquiry," Knox started.

She resisted the urge to snort at his unnecessarily elevated vocabulary.

"Some of my advisors have started questioning my judgment in light of my... interest in your specific case."

Verity heard her father grunt in warning but ignored him. Instead, she took a step closer to the glass. "That's it?"

He nodded.

"My daughter is the reason you lost control of your throne and we now have to fend off a violent alien invasion?"

She knew what he meant but she couldn't help be insulted at his wording. It sounded like he didn't think she was worth a war, and everyone had thought Helen of Troy was due to her beauty. Was it impossible to think that she could have the same influence?

Before Knox could answer, Verity asked her own question. "What does Arfilmea think about all of this?"

She ignored her father's questioning glance at the new name and waited for Knox to speak.

"She's taken Eiz'm's side."

"But he's not royal." The words were out of her mouth before she could stop them. It was an obvious statement but her reasoning had stayed completely internal. "What I mean to say is… she seemed very…"

"Power hungry?" Knox supplied.

She nodded. "If he's not the rightful ruler, why would she align herself with him?"

"We didn't see eye to eye on some important relationship aspects." His gaze pinned her to where she stood, making it clear she was, again, one of the reasons.

"She can't become queen if she broke your engagement, though."

"I'm sure she thinks he'll win. And she enjoys being the center of attention."

Yep. She was definitely part of their breaking up. A part of her was glad, because she didn't really like the female, but now that Knox was completely available… how was she going to resist him? She shouldn't want him at all, but that obviously hadn't stopped the attraction. His being promised to someone else had been a barrier in the back of her mind even if she didn't like to think about them as a couple. She was still scarred from catching them together.

"So, no one is loyal to you up there?" Verity's father cut in.

"I sent two of my agents to monitor it."

"Who?" she asked the same time her father asked, "What have they reported?"

"I haven't been able to reach either Trohm or Zeph," Knox admitted.

"Zeph?!" she exclaimed. Was she ever going to make friends with a guy who wasn't secretly an alien?

She turned to check on Hughes and McDonald who were guarding the door behind them. She hoped like hell she hadn't been duped twice more. But she didn't think so. They still emanated red and Knox and Dr. Makzik hadn't. And no one but Makzik knew she was having that symptom, so she had an upper hand in this apparent humanity test without them being able to intentionally deceive her.

But she'd definitely be slapping both Trohm and Zeph if she saw them again. It wasn't nearly a severe enough consequence for their betraying her trust but she wasn't going to delude herself into believing that she could make them suffer beyond that. And as angry as she was at them, she wasn't going to use her newfound knowledge of how to kill Eochronians against them. Because if Knox was right and they were his only allies left on the ship, she needed them alive.

She saw Knox smiling smugly.

"Now is not the time to be proud of your agents' ability to infiltrate us, so knock it off," she snapped.

His mouth flattened but his amusement remained obvious from the glint in his eyes.

She changed the subject. "What about Aerue?" she asked, remembering his—and her—guard's name.

He looked surprised that she remembered the name and she raised an eyebrow at him, insulted that he thought so little of her memory.

"I haven't been able to reach him. I'm sure Eiz'm is holding him captive."

"How do you know he isn't dead?"

"Because not even Eiz'm would kill Arfilmea's brother. Her support is strategic, and likely helped him win over any council members who may have been initially hesitant to become traitors."

Verity sighed. He was probably right. But as annoying as Knox and Aerue had both been to her on the ship, she didn't want anything bad happening to them at Eiz'm's hands. Or orders.

She wanted to kick herself. Deciding she needed them alive was one thing. Fearing for their actual well-being was another, and not something she should be indulging in.

"Do you have anything else to add?" her father asked, a sharp edge to his voice. "Or is that the extent of your help?"

She sensed his impatience at her back and tore her gaze away from the alien king.

But that didn't stop her skin from prickling with the heat of his stare on her.

"My kind eats and drinks like humans, but we need sunlight or other star light for energy. Without it, we become sluggish and eventually die."

"Then how are you still functioning right now?" she asked. He'd been stuck in the basement long enough that she expected him to look a little sick if he was telling the truth.

"I stockpiled energy before I was taken into custody." Knox didn't look at anyone in particular as he said the words but she flinched at the veiled accusation that she'd tricked him. "Even so, we can go for more than a single human day on a single 'charge.' But, of course, we burn energy faster when we're exerting ourselves."

Knox glanced at her as he finished and she fought a blush, thinking of a dirtier example than the conversation called for.

"And Eiz'm's army will likely have stockpiled energy in preparation for the battle."

He maintained contact with her as he spoke, and she forced herself to not fidget under his scrutiny.

Feeling like a coward again, she turned and walked away from the table without saying goodbye. As she passed her father, she saw some of the tension leave his shoulders, though he still wasn't relaxed even by its loosest definition.

Hughes and McDonald nodded at her and opened the door for her.

Verity heard Hughes calling for other guards to be dispatched to protect her father, saying he'd stay behind until they arrived.

She and McDonald raced up the stairs but she kept herself to a human pace, and they walked back to her home in silence.

At least until he spoke.

"You okay?"

"What do you mean?"

"You've been seeing him a lot. Just thought maybe..." he trailed off, clearly at a loss for words of how to express his concern further.

"I'm fine," she muttered, and pushed herself to walk faster, focusing on the stretching and contracting of her leg muscles with every step.

It was better than thinking about Knox and what his close proximity was doing to her.

25

KNOX

KNOX HAD WATCHED Verity leave with an uncomfortable amount of longing. It seemed she was always doing that, and he was growing to hate it more each time.

Hughes and her father remained, both frowning at him as usual.

"Well?" the general prompted again.

Knox hadn't responded to his earlier question since he'd been too busy watching Verity.

"I can contact my other agents who are still on Earth to advise your other countries on how to improve their defense plans. I would do the same if you let me."

"How and where are your moles?"

"In high enough positions to be listened to, though a good word from you would certainly help speed the communication process along."

"A good word?" The man said the words as if they were a foreign concept. "I'm not vouching for any of your kind, especially if I don't know who they are."

Knox sighed. "Do you want a list?"

"You have nothing to write with."

Knox didn't tell him he already had it written in Eochronian and it would be simple to convert to English and then display it through his armor.

The man would have to approach the glass, which Knox doubted he would do but it wasn't as if he were going to attack the general.

Without further prompting, Knox displayed the list to prove he was serious about helping. Actions spoke louder than words, as the human saying went.

The man came closer, surprising him, but Knox didn't move a muscle, not wanting to spook him or earn himself another shock from the collar.

Verity's father snapped a picture of the list with his phone then stored the device in his pants pocket.

Knox took it one step further and contacted his moles en masse and waited for them to appear before him. Again, he kept the projections in the human light spectrum.

One by one, they all appeared.

"Your Majesty," they greeted in unison.

"I need you to talk to the humans at the top about an impending invasion by Vruxols and potentially Eochronians."

Some looked surprised while others were better at keeping their reactions hidden behind a mask of calm.

"You want us to blow our cover, Your Majesty?" one timidly asked.

"Yes," he said. "And do it soon. I'll smooth the way for the humans to actually listen to you. But even if they don't, start building a detection shield so we know when they've entered the atmosphere. I don't want any more surprises."

"Yes, Your Majesty," the agent responded.

"That will be all," he said before ending the communication.

He saw the general staring at him with what looked like an impressed expression for the first time. It disappeared almost instantly.

"Will you contact their superiors?" Knox asked, keeping the frustration he felt at needing to out of his voice.

He wasn't enough of a dictator to take a lot of pleasure in issuing orders. Still, he did enjoy knowing that his words were interpreted as directives to be followed, rather than having to ask and appeal for favors in order for people to do what he wanted.

The general refused to give him the satisfaction of confirming he'd follow through on the request but Knox knew the man would. It would be stupid to do otherwise and they both knew it. The only thing the human seemed to take more seriously than protecting his daughter was protecting his planet.

An admirable trait.

And Knox could empathize. It was only circumstances that were forcing him to see some of his kind as an enemy. For his whole life up until this point, they had all been united. With the obvious exception of Eiz'm, of course.

The general seemed to be waiting for him to offer more but what was he expecting?

"That's all I can do from here," Knox said.

The promise that he could easily remedy that was left unsaid.

The human raised his head proudly and turned on his heel before striding out.

Though his walk was much more angular than his daughter's, Knox could easily see where she learned her attitude and swagger from. Well, him, and likely having been surrounded by rowdy men for most of her life.

He pushed the idea out of his mind. He didn't like thinking about how many likely were as hung up on her as he was, and wondering if she'd indulged any of them—aside from Trohm and her captain.

Just thinking about it still made him angry, but Trohm had seemed adequately repentant when he'd reprimanded him for taking such liberties with her. But even Knox knew that his agent likely cherished the experience and didn't regret a moment of it.

Once Knox got his chance, he would do the same, so he couldn't exactly blame Trohm.

Alone again, Knox let the hum of the security cameras lull him into a meditative state. It was better than outright boredom but only marginally so.

If only Verity had stayed longer to verbally spar with him. Or openly enjoy and practice her emerging Eochronian abilities. But he wouldn't have just viewed her as entertainment. He would have used the extended time with her to continue learning about her and trying to charm her.

With each encounter, she appeared more receptive to him, and he wanted to keep the momentum going.

He had been a fool to cut their kiss short after that meal together. Because even though he wouldn't have taken her fully like he had wanted to, and still desired to, he could have relished other sensual pursuits and experiences with her.

But because his self-control had been in charge at that moment, he only had his dream to hold him over until he could live it in reality.

26

VERITY

BEFORE THEY COULD OPEN her home's front door, McDonald pressed a hand to his earwig and cursed.

Verity listened to her father saying that the Aeronautical Space Exploration organization had urgently contacted the base with the news that something had entered the atmosphere and was headed right for them.

"I'll handle it, sir. Your daughter is safe with me." He tapped the earpiece once then turned his attention on her. "Get inside," McDonald whisper-yelled.

She rushed into the house and heard McDonald follow her in as he withdrew his gun from his holster.

"There's one inside the closet door," he said.

Verity ran to it and groped the small wall around the closet's frame until she came away with a .45. She checked to see it was loaded and cocked the gun, readying herself to fire if necessary. It wasn't the 9mm she had in her bedroom, but she was still comfortable with the different model. Her father had been insistent she learn more than one in case she didn't have access to any given weapon.

McDonald was coordinating with the other guards outside

her home and she heard them closing in. Well, she hoped it was them. She heard footsteps and hadn't yet figured out the difference between Eochronian and human ones.

Verity stayed behind McDonald as the door opened again, revealing Flynn and some other STFs. She took a deep breath and let herself relax a little.

She had the awful thought that one of them could still be an enemy Eochronian. They moved so fast, it was possible they had killed one of her guards and switched uniforms.

"All clear," Flynn said to McDonald.

"Nothing on the radar?" McDonald asked.

Flynn shook his head.

Before anyone could say more, the door burst open, revealing Trohm and Zeph.

Verity turned on the safety and slipped the gun in her waistband. She wasn't going to need it with these two. No, she had something else in mind. She stepped around her cadre of guards and slapped both of them at the same time with her hands. She wasn't ambidextrous but her anger was enough to guide her left hand with as much force and direction as her right.

Zeph seemed shocked while Trohm had the nerve to give her a lopsided smile.

"Knock it off, *Trohm*," she snapped. "Yeah, I know about you, too, Zeph," she added before he could ask why she'd also attacked him. "You're lucky you're not human or I'd already be putting you in the ground."

Trohm finally stopped smiling.

"How?" Zeph asked.

"Your king ratted you out. He's in custody," she explained while glaring at Trohm. "But he won't tell me why he's sticking around."

He and Zeph shared a knowing look and Verity felt her palms itch to hit them both again.

"Why are you here?" she demanded. "Shouldn't you be staging an unnecessary jailbreak for your king?"

"Eiz'm is almost ready to attack. We thought it best to help you defend your kind."

Verity still wasn't sure why Knox and his true supporters were so gung ho about protecting humanity but she wasn't about to complain. She still couldn't trust them but beggars couldn't be choosers. "What do you mean *almost*? He already has an army backing him. Why is he waiting?"

"There are a few hold-outs in the army and the Council."

"I'm sure Knox will be happy to hear that."

"It's not going to matter soon," Zeph said. "If they don't comply within the next twelve hours, they'll be executed. I doubt they'll wait that long, which means the attack could happen in the next minute."

She sighed and brushed past them through the front door, bumping both their shoulders as she did. "Coming?" she tossed over her shoulder before taking off at full speed toward Knox.

She heard them and her human guards following her, including Flynn's urgent call to her father.

This time, the guards didn't bother blocking her entrance and instead opened the doors for her. "Let the others in," she told them, rubbing the back of her neck the way she had when they agreed to let her in last time. She had no idea if that's what had made it work before but there wasn't any harm in trying.

They nodded without offering an objection so either they had decided it was easier to follow her orders or she had been right about activating the ability.

She ran downstairs and found Knox waiting in his seat with her father standing closer to the glass than she'd seen him do before.

He turned. "Verity—"

"Trohm and Zeph are here."

She barely got the words out before they appeared beside her.

"How did you run so fast?" Trohm asked her.

"As if you can't guess," she said, not bothering to look at him. Instead, she kept her gaze on Knox who seemed too entertained by seeing her with his two agents. He'd already admitted he was kinky when it came to bondage. Was he a voyeur, too? She pushed the idea out of her mind before she could start blushing.

"Say what you came to say," she said.

"Eiz'm will be attacking soon," Zeph said. "He's threatened to execute the last few soldiers and Council members who have resisted voicing their support for him. He gave them twelve hours from the time we left."

He left out the part where he assumed it wouldn't take that long, but by Knox's grim expression, the alien king understood it all the same.

Verity turned to see her father's reaction. His frown revealed how displeased he was by the turn of events but he didn't let any surprise he might be feeling show. She wasn't sure if anything could surprise him anymore after what had happened since the night she was abducted.

He pulled out his cell phone and angrily punched in some numbers.

She listened to him bark orders at his secretary—who definitely deserved a raise after putting up with all the recent, unexpected and late-night orders—to contact the world leaders and military personnel again, make sure they were listening to the alien moles from the list he'd sent her earlier, and to pull all STFs out of assignments to assemble in the training area.

She didn't have to check on the others in the room to know that every Eochronian was also eavesdropping.

"Is there something we should know?" Knox asked.

"I want you three to train my men to beat your turncoat brethren and your alien enemies."

"Vruxols," she corrected, earning a smile from Knox.

She gave a slight shake of her head. Now wasn't the time.

"Don't hold back on training them. They need to be prepared. But if you kill any of them, I'll kill you."

"Which one do you want?" Knox said. "You just gave us two contradicting instructions."

"Guess," her father growled.

"It's settled, then." Knox stood up suddenly, breaking the chains and entered the code to unlock the door behind him.

Verity held in her chuckle at her father's angry expression. They were all expecting it at some point but neither of them had anticipated seeing it in person.

A moment later, Knox came out of the wall's secret door and approached her slowly.

She saw her father reaching for the shock collar's remote. She waited until he pulled it out of his pocket and grabbed it.

"Verity!" he admonished.

She held it tightly, refusing to release it.

"Okay, now that we've agreed that they're going to train the STFs, let's stop wasting time here and get to it."

"Don't even think about—"

Verity ran off again before her father could finish issuing the order. Since she'd gotten used to speeding around with her newly enhanced senses, she'd finally stopped excessively sweating and returned to her natural inclination of anhidrosis. For most people, it was a scary medical condition but it had never been a problem for her and more of a blessing to avoid soaking all her dance and workout clothes.

Knox was beside her a second later, as were Zeph and Trohm who flanked them.

She ran to the front of the training area where her father had given more than a few addresses to the company. Some of the STFs reacted fast enough to pull a weapon but most were shocked at her sudden appearance with the three male aliens in tow.

The guns pointed away from her immediately but then aimed at her companions.

"I'm sure my father will address you once he arrives," she said, raising her voice as loud as possible so they could all hear her. "But there is an alien invasion that could happen in a minute or the next hour. In the meantime, they," she gestured to the men behind her, "are going to teach you how to fight the enemy aliens."

The STFs had obviously been training for this very occasion but they'd never had the opportunity to learn from the enemy. Well, knowingly, since many of them had trained with Trohm while he was pretending to be Tristan.

She finished just as her father entered the edge of the training area.

Verity could hear his hard breathing from where she stood, which meant Knox and his agents probably could, too. Her father wasn't out of shape but he had likely been pushing himself to his limit to make sure she hadn't been kidnapped again.

The STFs closer to her noticed her attention grabbed by something behind them and turned to watch her father make his way to the front.

You'd never guess how loud the group could get on a night out based on the deafening silence that currently filled the base.

When her father reached her, she moved aside to let him take the figurative spotlight.

"My daughter is correct. First, these... individuals," he practically choked on the word, "will give you a demonstration. Then I want you to divide into your teams and start fighting. Don't hold back. The aliens you'll be fighting are stronger, faster, and in some cases, larger."

Verity saw some of the STFs exchanging looks at each other, and heard one quietly mutter, "larger?"

She gestured to the Knox, Trohm, and Zeph. "They're Eochronians," she explained, jumping in before her father could continue his speech. "But another alien race, Vruxols, are supposedly bigger and more brawn than brains."

"Get creative and get dirty. And remember, you may be fighting more than one at a time. They," he gestured to the Eochronians, "will be making rounds and challenging you to fight a true alien."

Verity saw many glaring at Trohm with enough intensity to incinerate if that were possible.

"Why aren't they locked up?" one of them asked.

"Because it's pointless," Verity spoke up.

"They tried to kill us."

"No, they didn't," she corrected. "They're here to help but if you want to ignore it, then it'll be your funeral. Literally."

No one said anything else.

Her father stepped back and motioned for Knox, Trohm, and Zeph to take over.

"I want you at home, far away from the fighting," he growled at her. "And if you manage to talk your way around your guards again to disobey this order, they will be dishonorably discharged the moment we've defeated the alien army. Am I clear?"

Verity swallowed and nodded. She didn't want anyone getting in trouble for her.

She met McDonald, Hughes, and Flynn at the edge of the training area and they started back to her home. She heard her father telling Zeph that he also wanted the alien to consult with the human Cyber Dogs to maximize their technological defenses, too.

Verity didn't turn to glance over her shoulder until they were far enough away that she wasn't sure if Knox could see her. Knowing her luck, he probably still caught her final look before she faced forward again. She needed to leave all thoughts of him behind. She couldn't completely put him out of her mind just yet —that would have to wait until she was sure Eiz'm was no longer a threat to her and her planet. Verity needed to start getting into the habit of not letting Knox fill her every waking thought.

He was like an earworm that wouldn't go away, but he had to. Eventually. Right?

No sooner had the thought entered her mind, the ground rocked beneath Verity as a shockwave emanating from the training field reached her and her guards.

One glance up confirmed that the invasion had started. She hadn't expected to see so many hostile ships filling the sky, packed so tightly that they blocked sunlight from getting through. It was now almost as dark as a total eclipse. Only a few gaps existed between some ships that were rounded with a flat bottom. Larger from the round, Eochronian escape pod she'd hijacked with Ben which could only fit four individuals but smaller than the home ship where she'd been a captive. She couldn't tell much more from the ground but those were clearly Eochronian in comparison to the others featuring hard angles to cut the air.

For the humans, they wouldn't be able to see. Knox and his few allies wouldn't be able to recharge their bodies if they needed to. And fighting an army would definitely burn through anyone's energy stores.

Verity grabbed one of Hughes' extra knives from his belt and took off towards the field, ignoring the calls to stay away from the fight and go home. She was part alien, which meant she stood a better chance at fighting them than most of her father's men. She was going to help them, and no one was going to stop her.

Verity took in the scene before her.

Everyone was already engaged in battle. As her father had predicted, every STF was fighting multiple enemies. And losing. Except for a few who seemed to hold off their adversaries' blows enough to survive but failing to land any attacks themselves. Maybe they also had some alien DNA and that was helping them?

It didn't really matter. Sooner or later, they'd likely fall victim to the stronger enemy.

She couldn't find Zeph in the fray. Had he gone to the Cyber Dogs like her father had instructed or was he in the middle of one of the hordes of Vruxols? He had lied to her but a part of her hoped he was okay. For Alfie's sake, if for no other reason. Her friend had no idea his boyfriend was an alien secret agent but he'd definitely notice if he suddenly disappeared from his life and never returned.

The Vruxols were easily one-and-a-half times as tall as her, twice as wide as the Eochronians—who were all either as slim as her if not more so—and had a bluish-purple skin tone that reminded her of her favorite nail polish. That might have to change going forward. And something important Knox had failed to mention in his description of the enemy species... they had four arms instead of two.

Trohm and Knox were fighting with their backs to each other, rotating in tandem as if it were a choreographed dance. Every time an enemy came at them, one of them nailed them with a few stabs before moving out of the way before the enemy could retaliate.

Knox had a blade in one hand and what looked like a small gun in the other. He wasn't using it too often but when he did, a blaze of light emitted similar to a flamethrower but more blinding.

The screams from those hit made her wonder why he wasn't using it every chance he got but she figured he was conserving its energy. Was all Eochronian technology based on starlight? If so, that was a real design flaw. Whenever Earth rotated, half the planet was bathed in darkness at any given time.

She supposed their ship could always keep them near a star but they should have planned for scenarios like this where they had no viable energy source.

Verity shook herself. She wasn't there to just observe. She

scanned the distance between them. Could she reach them? She'd never used her alien speed with so many obstacles in the way.

Only one way to find out.

Hopefully she wouldn't get attacked on her way there. It was obvious human sight wasn't fast enough to target an alien moving at full speed, but she bet Eochronians and Vruxols had solved that hiccup when developing their arsenal.

Before she could talk herself out of it, she ran right for Trohm and Knox. The few times she did see an alien enemy close enough to her, she fired a shot from her gun or threw a random stab—depending which side they were on.

From their dismayed grunts, no one had been expecting her sneak attacks. By the time they realized what had happened, she had already moved far enough away that pursuing her would give the STFs an opening to attack.

"Verity—" Trohm started when she finally made it to them.

"Not now," she said. "Make room for me."

He did without asking, turning his body so there was enough space for her to squeeze her shoulders between his and Knox's to create a triangle.

She could feel the alien king's gaze on her but didn't acknowledge it. She couldn't afford getting lost in his eyes when they could all die at any moment.

"How many have you killed?" she asked them.

"Three?" Trohm guessed. "I haven't exactly been counting."

"Five," Knox corrected.

"Of course, he was," Trohm added.

Verity wasn't surprised. He seemed like a stickler for details.

Though she was a little surprised the count wasn't higher given how easily he had killed Dr. Makzik. Then again, she had been alone and not expecting his attack.

Verity saw an enemy approaching over Knox's shoulder and aimed her gun at the threat. She pulled the trigger and one bullet knocked the being out. She went to fire again but nothing came out. Shit.

Had she really gone through a whole magazine already? She hadn't thought she was being too generous with the bullets but she'd shot at least twice every time to do as much damage as possible.

She dropped it on the ground and kicked it into the triangle she had formed with Knox and Trohm. She didn't want an enemy grabbing it and filling it with some space bullet that was even deadlier.

"I only have one weapon," she said to them as they rotated and she blocked a Vruxol's blow with her left arm while plunging her knife upward into the gap between the helmet and chest plate. Thick, puce green liquid started dripping from the incision and dripped over her hand. She gagged and fought the urge to throw up.

She lunged forward, pushing the knife deeper and sliced to her right, nearly decapitating the Vruxol, who stumbled back, gurgling and grabbing its throat.

Now that she wasn't in immediate danger, she felt Knox press a handle into her left hand. A glance down revealed the item to be a long dagger that would let her attack while maintaining more distance than the blade she'd taken from Hughes.

Trohm's left shoulder pressed into hers and she took the hint to rotate.

She decapitated her next enemy so fast that another came at her before she, Trohm, and Knox repositioned themselves.

Out of her peripheral vision, she could see that a mix of Vruxols and traitor Eochronians were going after her two fighting companions but only Vruxols were coming her way. Perhaps they believed their size would easily subdue her. If she had been unarmed, they would have been right.

But she was surprising even herself by living out her super assassin dreams she'd been nurturing ever since watching a TV show about a female femme fatale. And here she was being a stone-cold badass in building her own pile of alien bodies.

But the body count didn't deter any of her attackers. They did start coming in pairs though, which made it harder to fight them since she couldn't retreat from their blows. It was the one downside of her formation with Knox and Trohm.

Since she was so much shorter than the Vruxols' height, she didn't have too hard a time ducking and avoiding SOME of their blows. But four fists—much less eight, when they double-teamed her—made it easier to trap her than just the two arms of the STFs or Knox during fight training. Soon enough, if she dodged one, she was hit by at least one other.

Her ribs were screaming with pain from each new blow. She was shocked they hadn't broken and punctured a lung yet. Or maybe it had and adrenaline was keeping her going. Verity knew she probably had to thank her messed up alien hybrid nature. If she survived this—and she'd fight like hell to make that happen— she'd probably have to thank her dad and Knox for doing it, though she wasn't going to let them forget that their methods still absolutely sucked.

Even as she was fighting the functionally faceless and neverending stream of enemies, she kept an eye out for one particular Eochronian.

She doubted she'd see his face in his armor. But she was convinced he'd still be recognizable by his single-minded hatred for Knox and, by some twisted extension, her.

No sooner had she thought about it than she recognized a blur of motion heading straight for them with so much force that it pushed the two Vruxols fighting her out of the way.

Clearly, Eiz'm didn't care much about the well-being of his army. They were just means to an end.

If only his minions would wake up to that fact and turn on him just like the hyenas had with Scar.

She wasn't that lucky. The aliens continued to target the few STFs who remained standing, and her trio.

Eiz'm and Knox broke away, attacking each other from every angle and both failing to gain the upper hand.

A moment passed and before she could brace herself, Eiz'm had shifted his attention to her. And then she was lifted into the air, tossed over his shoulder, and ran through the battlefield as if he were a quarterback gunning for a touchdown.

She heard the spaceship door shut behind them, trapping her with Eiz'm. He threw her down to the ground and she winced at the hard impact. Then she felt the cold manacles closing around her wrists.

A moment later, Eiz'm was gone, leaving her in the dark.

Out of the corner of her eye, she could see Aerue in a similar position on the other side of the large cell she had been thrown in.

He looked pale and almost gray. Sick, even. Was he dying?

Verity couldn't reach the door but she extended her arm as far as the chains would allow. But she touched an invisible divider instead. Luckily, it wasn't an electric barrier but it was solid. There was no way she was going to break through and get to Aerue.

"Why did he take me?" she wondered aloud.

"Because Knox cares for you," Aerue answered, his voice raspy. "And taking you hurts him. He may also use you for leverage."

"Knox is the rightful king. He won't surrender because of me."

"Won't he?"

She didn't answer.

"He cares for you. Is he alone in that?"

Verity took a deep breath. "No," she admitted. "But it's complicated."

"Well, you better figure it out fast before Knox makes an irreversible decision."

"What would you suggest, Arrow?" She knew it wasn't his name but the nickname slipped out. "It's not like I can send him a text message and let him know he should keep his crown instead of saving me." And she wasn't exactly sure she wanted to sacrifice herself for his position.

"We need to get out of here," Aerue said.

"No shit, Sherlock."

"Who?"

"Nevermind," she muttered. "Trohm was doing well with Knox when Eiz'm grabbed me. I think they're probably still okay."

Aerue sighed. "That's good." But he didn't offer any other words of encouragement.

Verity leaned back against the wall, letting her head fall against it and stare out into the dark corridor outside her cell. She should have appreciated the small, shitty room Knox had given her when she had the chance.

Because this was so much worse, and the one calling the shots was probably way too eager to see her dead than keep her alive for more scientific experiments.

She was screwed. In space. Again.

27

___

KNOX

KNOX NOTICED the line of Vruxols and traitor Eochronians forming to attack him. He pulled the trigger on his binary pistol and burned them as he scanned the crowd for Verity's father.

He spotted him on the far side of the field. He hadn't noticed the man move so far away but it was likely Eiz'm's directive to separate the humans from him and Trohm as much as possible. It would make it easier to pick off the humans since they wouldn't be able to protect them.

"You good?" he asked his loyal agent.

"Fine," he gritted out. "You gonna save the general?"

Knox took off instead of answering. As he passed enemies, he stabbed them, bringing most to their knees as he then severed them in half by dragging the blade through their torsos.

He wasn't as good a fighter as Aerue but his friend had trained him well enough to ensure he was still a lethal killing machine. His father had also been well-versed in combat though he, too, favored civil politics over brute force.

Knox reached the general and retracted the blade into his suit. He placed the handle of his pistol in his mouth to free both hands then snapped the neck of the Vruxol about to crush the human's head.

Verity's father raised his gun and shot Knox's chest point-blank. His armor easily shielded him from the attack but he still felt an impact.

"It's me," he said.

The human grunted and Knox wondered if the general had already guessed that before deciding to shoot. Now that he thought about it, that was probably the case.

"Where is the most secure location on base, sir?" Knox asked, tacking on the honorific to appease the man's pride.

"I'm not going to tell you."

"General, we don't have time to argue about this. Verity's been taken and I need to go rescue her. But I want to make sure you're safe first."

The man's hard expression turned into one of fear, and he didn't bother hiding it like his daughter regularly did. Maybe the general had realized it was pointless to put on an act for Knox when they both wanted Verity safe.

"Bunker underneath my office building," the general finally answered.

"Hold on," Knox commanded before he picked the man up, tossed him over his shoulders like a backpack, and ran to their destination.

Knox placed the man on his feet at the door and let him open the door. Knox followed him through security and together, they entered the same metal box as before.

Once the sliding doors closed, Knox watched the man insert a physical key into the button panel, revealing a hand and iris scanner.

Verity's father placed his right palm on the screen and brought his eyes close to the slot.

Knox watched the infrared and ultraviolet lasers verify his biometrics.

Then they shot downward for as long as it had taken to go up to the general's office.

They were now deep underground. Smart on the humans' part. Even without knowledge of his kind's need for star light, their safe haven made it impossible for an enemy Eochronian to survive for long. But Knox kept that information to himself. He didn't want the general deciding to shut him, Zeph, and Trohm down here once the Vruxols and Eiz'm's followers had been handled.

"Gather as many of your leaders down here as you can," Knox instructed. "And tell one of them to alert Zeph about the situation. He'll add extra security to the scanners so no one can force their way in here."

"Are you going after her now?"

"Yes, sir." He paused. "I am sorry for all of this."

Though he never would have met Verity had he not first experimented on his unborn daughter.

"How did Verity take learning about her hybrid nature?"

The man snorted. "Not well, though I wasn't expecting anything else from her."

Knox nodded in agreement. "Stay safe, sir."

"Bring her back to me in one piece."

He doubted dismemberment was on Eiz'm's agenda, but he knew the human phrase meant healthy and safe rather than its literal meaning. "I will, sir."

He called the metal box by pushing the singular button next to the doors and climbed back inside. There were clearly no security measures in place on LEAVING the secret bunker, but he supposed its priorities were in order. Theoretically, if someone unverified managed to get down there, them returning to the surface wasn't as much of a worry.

Knox tapped out a message to Zeph as he exited the base, telling him to do all he could to protect the humans with the help of the technological unit. He'd already left Trohm on the battlefield to do the same, albeit in a different manner. Knox didn't need Verity getting mad at him for her father getting injured or killed in his absence.

Once he was half a mile outside the front gate, Knox called his ship to him. He hadn't done it while inside because he didn't need any of Eiz'm's soldiers destroying his private ship.

The moment it finished forming, he unlocked the pod and climbed in and set the navigation back to the mothership. All the escape pods were tied to its location the same way they were linked to an individual Eochronian's armor.

He accelerated and launched into space.

Hold on, Verity, he thought, as if she could hear his thoughts. *I'm coming to get you.*

28

VERITY

VERITY DIDN'T REMEMBER DOZING off but the sound of her cell opening woke her.

A broad Eochronian stood over her and released her from the wall before attaching another set of cuffs to her wrists.

He was bigger than Aerue and had clearly taken over his job as main guard under Eiz'm's regime. Which made him an ass for going against Knox. He had a sorry expression on his face as he took her, so he was an apologetic ass instead of a full-blown asshole. But still an ass, all the same.

He stopped in front of a door and murmured, "I'm sorry," before pushing her into the room.

The same interrogation room she'd been in last time with both Eiz'm and Aerue.

But now that Aerue was imprisoned and Knox wasn't even onboard, Verity knew she was in for a violent beating with no end in sight.

Eiz'm came up behind her and forced her into the chair, binding her to it even tighter than he had before. Her chest was being crushed so badly it was hard to take in a shallow breath, let alone a deep one that would help mitigate the forthcoming pain.

"Why are you doing this?" she asked.

His answer was a right hook to her jaw.

It hurt less than when he'd done the same thing to her during her first captivity. Which meant she probably had her growing alien side to thank. Too bad she wasn't as strong as Knox and his friends to break out of the chair.

Then again, this chair could probably hold any alien species, including Eochronians. If it couldn't it would be pointless.

"Do I need to say anything or are we going to skip past the part where we pretend you want anything from me other than my pain?"

Any information he needed about her father's base was probably already leaked by Dr. Makzik. He hadn't injected her with the truth serum either.

This time, he punched her cheekbone.

She was lucky it didn't hit her eye but she doubted that would remain the case.

Verity bit her lip until she tasted blood, focusing on that pain instead of the stinging aches radiating from where he'd targeted.

Would holding her breath again until she passed out work? The drowning had clearly been a test to see how effective their experiment on her was progressing, and she'd lasted a while then. Now that she was even more transformed, it would probably take even longer. And by that point, Eiz'm would have dealt extra damage that made her wonder if the likely brain damage from lack of oxygen was worth it.

Probably not.

Which meant she was going to have to endure everything he decided to dole out without a backup plan to get out of it.

Eiz'm continued to rain blows down on her, alternating between slaps and punches. Assuming he didn't outright kill her before this was over, she was going to wake up tomorrow as one giant bruise.

Verity took each hit without complaint. She refused to give

him the satisfaction. But inside, she was crying and cursing with every impact.

She'd started bleeding after the fifth blow, and while some wounds were still flowing, she could also feel her hair and parts of her skin tightening under dried blood. Keeping track of the number of hits was the only thing keeping her alert. While she had decided against forcing herself to pass out, she didn't want to lose her bearings around Eiz'm.

The bastard would take any weakness and use it to his advantage. She didn't want to think about what his sadistic imagination would come up with. So, she wouldn't give him the chance.

But her lack of reaction appeared to also enrage him and soon he surprised her by removing her from her restraints and slinging her limp body over his shoulder.

Eiz'm must have done something to expand the room because suddenly he roughly threw on her a large, hard table. Understanding and terror seized her.

The need to survive gave her a surge of energy to fight back. She kicked him and tried to flip over on her hands and knees to crawl away but he stopped her.

He grabbed her ankles, wrenched her pants down, and forced her legs open. Then he climbed on top of her and settled between her thighs.

He wasn't naked yet but she knew what was coming.

Verity decided to try a different tactic and hooked her leg around his and twisted her hips, trying to flip them.

He didn't budge.

The romance novels she'd read had made it seem so much easier to flip a man but they were all playful scenes and involved two consenting parties. This was different. And he wasn't human.

Verity refused to freeze and surrender but nothing she was doing was helping.

Realistically, she wasn't going to escape this but she still resisted adopting a defeatist attitude. It was a sure way to lose in any situation. But since there was no winning for her now, the principle was all she could cling to.

He ripped her shirt down the middle, completely baring her to his predatory gaze.

As she anticipated, things got even worse.

Like his other torture of her, he was hard and cruel in his abuse.

She shut her eyes and didn't bother trying to hide the tears or her cries of pain. No one was going to help her but she couldn't stop them, and there wasn't much point in pretending that Eiz'm wasn't winning.

Verity didn't know how long it lasted. She didn't want to.

But he finally stopped, he sneered in her ear, "He won't want you now, will he?"

When he pulled away and she could no longer hear him nearby, she curled in on herself and tentatively opened her eyes and noticed Arfilmea in the doorway.

A perverted reverse of when she'd caught her with Knox.

The woman stood stiffly and had a stricken expression, her eyes wide with alarmed shock and her facial muscles pulled tight. Verity thought she saw remorseful tears shining in her eyes before Arfilmea turned away.

Verity wanted to ask if she was happy with choosing Eiz'm over Knox but her throat was sore from her screams.

The large guard from before walked past the open doorway and froze when he took in her naked form.

He turned around and walked back the way he'd come. A few moments later, he returned and sat on the edge of the table where she'd been left like a gutted animal in a science experiment.

Verity flinched, but he gently dressed her in clothes, being sure his hands didn't linger any longer than strictly necessary. She looked down and saw that she was wearing her old pajamas.

Verity refused to think too much about why both Knox and Eiz'm wouldn't have destroyed them once she escaped.

Once she was fully covered again, the guard lifted her into his arms, cradling her like a child, and walked her back to her cell.

It was just as cold and unforgiving as before but she welcomed it if it meant she didn't have to be with Eiz'm.

But she wouldn't let herself depend on it. Because this was likely only a brief respite from her tormentor.

"I am sorry," he said again, as he chained her back up—a little looser this time around.

Not enough for her to escape but the cuffs no longer painfully dug into her skin.

Verity wasn't sure how to feel about that. It might give her something to focus on instead of the ugly memories that were already surfacing. She'd somehow managed to partially dissociate during the assault but now that she was essentially alone again— Aerue hadn't responded to her return and she wondered if he was sleeping—her mind was turning against her after her body already failed her. Again. With worse consequences than when it had let her down with the first alien contact.

Some time later, Aerue finally spoke up. "Are you okay?"

Verity lifted her head off her shoulder and saw Aerue watching her from his cell.

She shook her head.

No. She was definitely not.

But she wasn't mad at him. He probably had no idea about what had happened to her. She didn't expect him to since he'd almost certainly been locked up here the whole time. If he had been removed and restored before her, he was most likely also tortured. She doubted he'd been thinking of her then.

Verity forced words out. "Do you Eochronians have special healing abilities, or something?" Her voice was raspy and pained both her throat and ears.

Despite his fatigue, Aerue managed a small smile in the dark.

"We do heal a bit faster than humans but nothing like you're thinking."

Dammit.

She sighed. If her new DNA couldn't help her, she wished she at least had Knox's fancy gold serum that had healed her after Eiz'm's attention as mere interrogator.

Verity desperately wanted to sink into the oblivion of sleep to escape her current reality but knowing her luck, she'd only relive the nightmare on a loop if she closed her eyes.

She never wanted to be a damsel in distress. Her father had trained her to never become one.

But here she was.

Knox, she thought, *where are you?*

29

KNOX

KNOX PARKED his pod in the hangar without issue.

Eochronian technology recognized its brethren and didn't raise an alarm. But someone monitoring the ship would still have seen him entering.

Which meant this was probably an ambush. And he was likely about to be swarmed with soldiers the moment he left the cockpit.

Knox readied his binary pistol and increased the lateral range so he'd be able to take out more guards at once, rather than just a bunch who were stupid enough to line up behind each other.

He tapped his armor to extend a blade. Unlike the one he was fighting with on Earth, however, he also made it binary-powered, and longer. He hadn't wanted to make the weapon so lethal earlier in case he accidentally injured one of the humans but now that possibility was removed.

Knox sighed. He'd procrastinated for as long as possible. Now it was time to fight. It broke his heart to have to cut down so many of his own soldiers. Well, they had been his. Their choice to defect had sealed their fates but he still mourned the loss of life.

He opened the door to the pod and jumped out before anyone

could crowd him into the confined space. And he started attacking immediately. Sometimes offense was truly the best defense.

His actions landed him a few wins on the enemies closest to him but most of the others only retreated a few steps.

More than enough for him to get out from being backed up against the pod. Now, he was on the outside of the group rather than being surrounded by them.

With every move, he swung his blade over his head and around his back to keep anyone from going behind him.

His binary weapons luckily kept everyone far enough away that very few were able to land harmful blows on him. Unfortunately, they also often successfully danced out of the way whenever he tried to retaliate.

Impatient to find Verity, he started using the pistol more liberally. He didn't have time to dodge and fight all of them indefinitely so he also started holding the trigger long enough each time to incinerate rather than merely burn his adversaries.

But the numbers kept coming. It seemed that Eiz'm was smarter than he assumed by keeping an ample supply of Eochronians on the ship to fight him. Now that he thought about it, most of the soldiers he'd fought on Earth had been Vruxols.

Though he would have assumed that keeping the Vruxols on the ship to keep the rest of the Eochronians in line while letting their kind fight humans would have made more sense. Aside from Verity, any human didn't stand a chance against an Eochronian and he'd seen that reality as the humans on the base had easily fallen.

He wasn't going to complain about not having to go up against the superior fighters now. Vruxols had been targeting Verity but only traitors had been going after him and Trohm. Though he had been successful in fighting them off, after all of that, if he had to battle Vruxols to get to Verity, he would probably be too fatigued to escape with her. Eiz'm had blocked sunlight from reaching the with all the ships so Knox had been unable to recharge. So had his enemies, but they hadn't been using their stores to survive in a basement like he had.

Even though they were more evenly matched than Vruxols, this skirmish was taking longer than he wanted it too. If this didn't resolve itself soon, he might have to take his chances in running around them and hope he got to Verity before they captured him.

Knox heard a door open but refused to check who entered. Whoever it was definitely wasn't on his side.

But the mystery appearance made everyone freeze, then stand at attention.

Knox turned to see Arfilmea standing in the doorway.

"I'll take it from here," she decreed.

The guards hesitated but eventually filed out, leaving the two of them alone.

What was happening?

She grabbed his hand and led her to her bedroom.

Before he anticipated her intentions, she pushed him down on the bed and climbed on top of him.

Knox flipped her before she could get comfortable. Then he climbed off the bed, putting as much distance between them as possible without going back into the corridor.

Realistically, Eiz'm already knew he was on board but he didn't know if his rival knew *where* he currently was.

"What are you doing?" Knox asked.

"I've missed you," she said, evading the question. She stepped forward and smoothed her hands down his chest before cradling his face and kissing him.

He jerked back and grabbed her shoulders, holding her at arm's length.

"Arfilmea," he said sharply. "Answer the question."

"I want to pick up where we left off."

"You're engaged." To a traitor, but he left that part unsaid.

Even if she weren't, he wouldn't go after another's partner. Infidelity was unacceptable in their culture, though open relationships were known to happen. After all, he and Arfilmea had planned for that before she'd broken it off.

"I'm just trying to survive, Knox," she said, her body softening under his grasp. "You weren't here to see the damage he was doing because you were too preoccupied with the human."

He finally let go of her, hoping she'd respect his personal space now.

"What about your brother?" he asked. If she was truly merely trying to survive, why hadn't she tried to get the same deal for Aerue?

"He's imprisoned because of his loyalty to you but alive because Eiz'm promised me not to hurt him."

"And you believe him?" If—by some miracle—his best friend was still alive, Knox doubted he was unharmed.

A look of uncertainty clouded his ex's features but it disappeared too quickly for his words to have changed her mind.

And there was still a glint of determination in her eyes that made him uneasy. She still had something planned she hadn't revealed and his gut told him it wasn't good for him.

That's when he noticed the small dagger. It was small, cylindrical, and too thin for a human to notice.

If he hadn't pushed her off him each time, he probably would have died with her lips on his. He internally shuddered but grabbed her wrist with one hand and the blade with the other. His armor prevented him from getting cut but he would have done it even if he hadn't been wearing it because an injury on his hand would heal. Being stabbed in the heart or brain wouldn't.

Using both hands, he wrenched the weapon away while also elbowing her in the chest, sending her back a step.

He had always agreed with Aerue that she should have learned some fighting skills alongside them as a precaution but now he was grateful she had always refused.

Knox absorbed the weapon into his armor so she wouldn't be able to take it back.

Then he swiped his leg underneath her feet and dropped her to the ground. He could have pushed her to the bed and then tied her up but he was so pissed he didn't care about cushioning the impact.

She glared up at him as if he were the one in the wrong.

He refused to be guilted, then decided to chain her to her bed all the same.

At least then she wouldn't be able to run back to Eiz'm and let him know her mission had failed. He gagged her, too, just to be safe.

It would hopefully buy him enough time to find Verity. Was she being held in the prison cells near Aerue? Or had Eiz'm decided to keep them both in unexpected sections of the ship? It would be a demented version of the human childhood game hide and seek.

Though he doubted Eiz'm had actually anticipated him surviving to even search for his friend and Verity.

Edging near the entrance of Arfilmea's room, he checked to see if any guards were patrolling the hall. None were.

He made a run for the long-abandoned jail cells. His father had barely used them and he hadn't needed to use it at all. Perhaps throwing Eiz'm in there sooner would have avoided this whole debacle.

Knox had vowed to not emulate his grandfather but he had to admit his ruthlessness had been a good deterrent to potential traitors. His father had inspired loyalty to not need fear as a weapon. Knox thought he had done the same but Eiz'm's success at turning the council and enough soldiers against him even before bringing in the Vruxols made Knox wonder if he'd been wrong in that assumption.

In hindsight, it seemed conceited to assume they would be loyal to him merely because he was their king and the son of their former leader. And he had made life much less luxurious in order to conserve their supplies with the goal of settling on Earth. Which the council certainly hadn't agreed with. No one but Aerue seemed to back his more progressive style of ruling despite his repeated attempts at making them see that he wasn't going to force Arfilmea into motherhood sooner than she was ready, and that forcibly taking over a planet might give them more resources but not a way to replenish their population without perpetuating the inbreeding that had already happened during his grandfather's generation. If he were willing to pursue that as a solution, they didn't need a new planet for that, though his council wouldn't listen to that logic. Their stubborn refusal to let go of their ideas and acknowledge the merit of his was frustrating but he respected the fact everyone deserved to have their own opinion, even when it contradicted his own.

All the same, their outright rebellion couldn't be forgiven. Each member of the king's army and the royal council had taken an oath to protect him and his lineage.

He reached the cells and thoughts of insufficient levels of loyalty faded as he took in the prone and injured forms of Aerue and Verity.

His friend was ashen gray. Knox wondered how long he'd been without starlight but it was obviously too long. He'd die within a month if this kept up. But the bruising on his ribs and face meant his body was using up its energy to heal him, which shortened the projected survival time by weeks.

Knox broke the lock and released Aerue, shouldering his friend's weight as he broke the lock on Verity's. He helped his friend to sit on the ground then turned his attention to Verity.

Her face was so bruised she was almost unrecognizable. But what was more appalling was the complete lack of alertness and expression of resignation she wore. Her blonde hair looked dull and knotted, so different from how neat and sleek she normally kept it.

It was as if the light had been snuffed out of her.

The sight broke his heart and also made a band of red rage tighten around his temples and cloud his vision.

He took his healing serum and applied some to Aerue before applying a bigger amount to Verity. It was already starting to clear up her face and she finally opened her eyes.

They widened with recognition but then drooped again. She was clearly still taxed and worn out from whatever torture she'd endured.

Eiz'm would pay for what he'd done to her. There was no question the asshole had personally tormented her. Slow and torturous rather than fast and furious, though Knox knew it would be a struggle to keep that instinct in check. And then Knox would kill him. And enjoy it.

Did that make him sick? Perhaps. But he wasn't going to apologize or make excuses for his desire for revenge in the name of avenging the two people who meant the most to him. Verity had taken that spot without trying, and he was done with ignoring the indisputable fact.

He undid her chains and gently lay her over his shoulder so he could also help Aerue up. He didn't trust his friend's ability to walk though his head guard shook off his offered hand and started walking on his own.

Knox switched Verity's position to cradle her and she wrapped her arms around his neck before burying her face into his neck. He didn't let himself enjoy her seeking comfort from him. They still needed to get out of here.

And then he saw Eiz'm standing right outside the cell, waiting for him.

Before he could stop him, Eiz'm knocked Aerue to the ground and the distraction loosed Knox's hold on Verity.

Eiz'm grabbed her, spun her around so she was staring at Knox. He could see the panicked look in her eye while Eiz'm's forearm almost choked her.

Knox started to move forward.

"Ah ah ah." Then the asshole pulled out a syringe filled with bright red liquid and aimed it at her neck. "Think about the consequences."

Knox forced his muscles to relax so Eiz'm would think he wasn't about to attack.

"What is that?" He kept his voice level.

"She interests me. I wonder what would happen if we finish what you started. It might kill her. On the other hand, she might become one of us."

"Wouldn't the success of my plan undermine your plan to seize power?"

Eiz'm tilted his head. "You like her humanity."

It wasn't a question so Knox didn't respond.

"If it's successful, she will lose that. And so will you."

He was willing to give up power just to personally hurt him? "Do you hate me that much?"

"You had everything handed to you," Eiz'm snarled. "You're soft and don't deserve to rule."

Knox stared at the needle then at Verity.

She'd gone stiff in Eiz'm's grasp and looked like she wanted to cry. More than that, she appeared to be trying to shrink into herself.

Whatever Eiz'm had done to her was more than hit her face. And if his sneaking suspicion was right, Knox now wanted to eviscerate him and feed him his own inner organs.

"If you had sped up her treatment, maybe she wouldn't be in this vulnerable position."

While Verity had been growing more comfortable with her speed and strength after some disastrous false starts, Knox doubted she'd be ready to fight Eiz'm even as a full-blooded Eochronian.

Eiz'm was trying to shift the blame on him for Verity's pain but Knox knew better than to be guilt-tripped. There was only one villain here, and it wasn't him.

But he couldn't take the chance that Eiz'm would follow through on his threat, so here they stood at an impasse with Verity's life in the balance.

He never should have entered her life. Knox saw that now. But it was too late for that. He would save her, somehow, and then leave her alone. She deserved that much, and much more.

30

VERITY

VERITY COULD FEEL the needle pressing into her neck even though Eiz'm had yet to press the plunger. She almost wished he would because then she wouldn't be thinking about him putting his hands on her again. The thought made her retch, and then she felt herself vomiting over herself and Eiz'm's arm.

He let go, uttering a non-human curse.

She hadn't done it to make him release her, though dropping to the ground was a self-defense method she'd learned because it caught a captor off guard. But now that his grip had loosened, she grabbed the needle from him and stabbed him with it, pressing the plunger until all of the red liquid had disappeared into his neck.

He crumpled to the ground and she stepped back in case he was acting.

Knox wrapped his arm around her waist and she focused on the fact it was him and not her tormentor, but her skin still felt like it was on fire from where Eiz'm had touched her—which had been everywhere.

Tears sprung to her eyes but she swiped at them angrily.

"Let's get out of here," Knox said, lifting her into his arms.

She saw Aerue standing and a collection of particles coalescing around him.

When the helmet closed over his head, Verity realized it was a suit of armor. Like the one Knox had been wearing while on Earth. She could feel it against her body but it wasn't hard like the body armor her dad's STFs.

Together, the three of them started running. Aerue ran next to Knox, who cradled her tightly in his arms.

A group of guards came at them.

"Can you stand?" Knox asked her.

Verity nodded, and he put her feet on the ground. She wobbled at first and he reached out to steady her. She took a deep breath and forced herself to focus. Knox couldn't fight these guards off while holding her, and Aerue wasn't back to full capacity.

She needed to help as much as possible. She just hoped she could regain her strength. None of them needed her as a liability.

The need to survive finally fired up what adrenaline her body had left.

Without a weapon, the best Verity was able to do was punch guards or hold them for Aerue or Knox to kill them. She wasn't strong enough right now to even knock the enemy soldiers out.

Even so, the unbalanced system she and the two aliens had created seemed to be working. The soldiers were slowly dwindling in number.

Unless Knox had failed to mention an Eochronian ability to change appearance, the giant guard who had taken her to and from her cell was noticeably absent. The soldiers here were all closer to Knox's height, making it an almost even fight for him and still gave a somewhat-injured Aerue an upper hand based on his size.

Was the giant caught up in other business or was his absence a choice? If so, why had he supported Eiz'm in keeping her prisoner but not attempting to prevent her escaping with Knox? Was the return of the true king that intimidating to him? Was it naïve of her to wonder if seeing her violated had triggered a change of heart in him?

Regardless of the reason, not needing to fight him made their escape that much easier.

But then Eiz'm appeared at the end of the hall. He didn't look any different, right down to the murderous gleam in his eye, but something had definitely changed since they'd last seen him. The injection had an effect. She just didn't know what it was.

Verity felt a blade being pressed into her hand and hid it by aligning it with her forearm. She met Knox's gaze and even though his expression gave nothing away, she knew he had done it just as he had on Earth. She probably wasn't lucky enough for the exchange to be unnoticed by Eiz'm but on the off chance he didn't realize she was now armed, maybe she'd get to surprise him.

And then he revealed the answer by moving so fast that he actually disappeared from her vision. When Knox and his kind moved quickly, she had still been able to see them as blurred figures once the alien DNA had started affecting her more. If he was faster, she could only assume he was also stronger.

She should have let him follow through on his threat and inject her with the serum instead. Maybe then she wouldn't be a weak half-human while fighting the best trained alien fighters.

This time when he made a grab for her, she tried to dodge but it wasn't enough. And he grabbed her head with both hands. One twist, and her neck would be broken.

"Wishing you hadn't attacked me, huh?" Eiz'm whispered in her ear.

She suppressed the urge to shiver in fear and disgust. If he knew how much he still scared her, he'd draw out this torture. But maybe that wouldn't be a bad thing right now. If he was too busy gloating about how he'd triumphed over her, maybe he wouldn't notice her shifting her grip on the weapon Knox had passed her.

Aerue and Knox were done fighting the other guards and now circled Eiz'm from both sides. Her captor kept her in front of him as a shield and regularly rotated to keep both men in his peripheral vision.

Verity took a deep breath and thrust the blade upward into the space between Eiz'm's ribs.

He didn't let go of her but he did stumble back a step.

Then his hands were wrenched away from her by Aerue and Knox. She turned around and grabbed the handle of the blade, withdrawing it and stabbing him again now that she could see her target. His arms were currently being stretched out to his sides, allowing her to go after him without his being able to defend himself. She wasn't going for the kill right now but just inflicting as many injuries as possible. It was nothing like what he'd done to her but she let herself enjoy exacting her revenge.

But then Eiz'm shook off both Knox and Aerue and lunged at her, gripping her hand so tightly she had to drop the blade.

Before he could escalate his attack, however, hands reached around his head and then his neck was snapped to the side.

His body dropped to the ground again, revealing Knox, but this time the asshole was dead.

Or, at least, Verity hoped he was. Snapping an Eochronian's neck had been enough to kill Dr. Makzik but there was a scary chance that the red serum had acted like at least one version of vampirism where a broken spine wasn't a permanent death.

Knox picked up the blade she'd dropped from the ground, pulled Eiz'm up by his hair, and slit the asshole's throat to the point of almost decapitating him.

Verity let out a breath. At least now it was clear he wouldn't be surprising them with another miraculous revival.

Seeing Knox's ruthless side should have scared her since his eyes now contained a glimmer of sadism. But it cleared as soon as he turned his attention from the dead body to her. His gaze softened immediately and became alarmed when the adrenaline suddenly left her, causing her to sway forward.

He caught her in his arms and his hands touched her shoulders, righting her again.

She stared up at him, silently asking the question she couldn't voice: What happened between them now?

Aerue walked up to them and cleared his throat. "Your Majesty, should you not handle the situation on Earth?"

Knox's gaze scanned her face.

She didn't know what he was looking for but after a few moments of inspection, he turned to his head guard, then touched his throat and tapped three times.

His voice boomed throughout the ship as he announced Eiz'm's death and issued the command to stand down against humans. He continued to instruct the soldiers to now defend against any living Vruxols. Once Earth was secure again for humans, all Eochronians were to return to the mother ship.

At the end of his short speech, Knox tapped his throat again and Verity somehow knew that he had gone off speaker mode, for lack of a better term.

"Keep an eye on the situation," Knox told Aerue, who nodded and walked away, stepping over the bodies of the fallen soldiers.

Verity took in the carnage around them. "I'm sorry."

"What for?"

"You've killed so many of your own kind to protect me."

He made a noncommittal sound in his throat.

"You're going to lie to me now and tell me your super-secret plan wasn't some sort of population control?"

He gave a wry smile. "Guilty. But they sealed their own fates when they turned against me."

"Still..." Verity trailed off. There wasn't anything else to say but staying silent after such a severe comment seemed wrong.

Knox was watching her again.

"What?" she asked.

"Are you okay?"

Verity nodded stiffly. His serum had helped her heal and Eiz'm hadn't physically hurt her again either time he grabbed her though she still wanted to scrub herself clean until she couldn't feel his touch on her. But she also didn't have the energy to take a shower, either here or in her bathroom on Earth—and who knew when that would be.

He must have seen something in her expression because Knox suddenly scooped her up and started walking.

"Put me down!"

"I'm taking you to be checked out by Dr. Mak'en. Then we can take you back home."

Home. Earth. It was hard to believe it had only been hours since she was there. So much had happened since then. More than what had during her month-long stay under Knox's orders.

The thought made her wrap her arms around his neck.

He glanced down at her but didn't comment on the move.

Verity didn't know what she would have said if he had. After everything that had happened between them, she still wasn't sure how to feel about the alien king. Attraction, frustration at said attraction, gratitude for his saving her, and anger at getting her into this mess with Eiz'm were all mixed together in a confusing and volatile emotional cocktail. She had no idea which emotion was driving her anymore but she was worried that any action she took would be driven by the wrong one. Probably a lose-lose situation in hindsight, even if she enjoyed her choice in the moment.

She clung to him as he walked down a number of different hallways until he finally entered the medical room she'd visited multiple times after her daily endurance tests.

Dr. Mak'en and her assistant looked up in surprise at the two of them.

Could they be trusted? Had they expected Knox and her to be killed? Hoped for it, even? It didn't look like Eiz'm had brutalized them in any way so maybe they had been okay with the coup?

Did it matter now that he was dead?

Knox lay her down on the medical table but she gripped his hand before he could step away.

He looked down at her and squeezed her hand in reassurance before recapping what had happened and instructing the doctor to inspect and heal her.

Dr. Mak'en moved a screen closer to her and scanned the length of her body, frowning at whatever it revealed.

Verity had the sinking feeling the woman knew that more had happened that Knox didn't know about.

Dr. Mak'en addressed her. "On a scale of one to ten, how much pain are you in?"

Verity almost laughed. She hadn't heard that question since she was a child and Dr. Lane asked that when she'd had a particularly bad fall. Well, not really Dr. Lane but Dr. Makzik. Verity sucked in a breath. Had her doctor on Earth and the one here been sisters? Their names were similar. And they bore some resemblance to each other. How had she missed it before?

"Verity?" the woman prompted.

"Eight," she finally admitted, unable to meet Knox's surprised gaze. It wasn't everywhere but definitely her ribs and hips, and wrists, where Eiz'm had bruised her with his unforgiving grip.

"Global pain or localized?"

Verity answered, staring at the ceiling instead of anyone else in the room.

The woman gave her a sympathetic look, understanding what she'd left unsaid.

Knox's hand had grown stiffer in her hand and she assumed he was starting to get the picture if he hadn't already figured it out.

"Would you like a full exam?" Dr. Mak'en asked, her gaze jumping between her and Knox.

"It's up to her," Knox replied tightly.

Verity knew the woman probably meant well but she didn't want anyone touching her. She shook her head and the doctor nodded.

"Very well."

The doctor's assistant handed her what looked like an airbrush gun with the gold healing liquid loaded into its chamber.

"This should only take a few minutes," Dr. Mak'en said as she started to spray Verity, pushing her clothes out of the way to get to the bruised areas but never fully undressing her and very quickly covering her back up after treating each section.

Then the doctor pulled a small tablet out of her coat pocket and scanned her body.

"What are you doing?" Verity asked.

"Checking for internal bleeding."

Something about her tone made Verity wonder what she was holding back. "And?"

"Signs of pregnancy."

Verity heard Knox emit a low growl but she just stared at the doctor. They could tell that fast?

"Are there?" Knox demanded.

Dr. Mak'en shook her head and Verity let out a sigh of relief.

"And the internal bleeding?" Verity asked. She didn't want to arrive home only to possibly die from not being treated.

"None that I can see," the woman replied, stowing the device.

It wasn't a perfect guarantee but she trusted that if the advanced Eochronian technology couldn't detect an issue, neither would the medical machines on Earth.

Dr. Mak'en addressed Verity again. "I know you likely want to return home but I recommend you get some rest before undertaking the journey."

Where was she supposed to do that? She refused to go back to the cell Eiz'm had kept her in, and even the small room Knox had assigned her. She doubted anyone with a comfier bed would be willing to give it up to her. Verity glanced at the alien king, checking to see his opinion on the medical advice.

"How long does she need to rest?"

"A few hours at minimum, Your Majesty. Her body has been going through a lot of changes lately, and I see that continuing for the foreseeable future. Not to mention the trauma she's recently endured." She turned her attention to Verity again. "I'd like to check you out one more time before you leave, as well. Just to be sure everything is in order."

He nodded, and held out his hand to Verity.

She placed hers in his and accepted his help in standing.

Together, they left the medical room and started walking toward his suite, his hand at the small of her back but not actually touching her.

He ushered her into the room and underneath his blankets on his spacious bed.

She stared up at him. Was he going to join her? Did she want him to?

"Go to sleep, Verity," he said, answering the question in her eyes. "I'll keep watch outside and make sure no one disturbs you."

Verity watched him walk to the door then found her voice. "Wait."

He stilled but didn't turn to face her. "Yes?" he asked softly.

"Please don't leave," she said.

"I want to give you space," he said.

She took a deep breath. "Your bed is big enough for both of us. I'm sure you need rest too."

He didn't argue but quickly climbed under the covers. She watched him turn his back to her, and she stared at him for a moment.

How badly had he been hurting but hiding from her?

A wave of exhaustion hit her, and she yawned. Turning over to give him her back, too, she burrowed further under the blankets, brought her knees up into fetal position, and let her head sink into the pillow.

She closed her eyes and willed the sleep to take her and prayed for no nightmares to haunt her.

31

KNOX

KNOX FELT something soft against his side. He opened his eyes and saw Verity curled against him.

He hadn't meant to actually fall asleep next to her but the tension of fighting Eiz'm and reclaiming his throne had tired him out more than he expected. He hadn't needed to dip into the solar reserves of his suit during the battle but if it had drawn out much longer, his good luck would have run out.

When he'd seen the bruises on Verity, he'd wanted to kill Eiz'm all over again but her uncharacteristically meek demeanor made him keep his anger at bay. He didn't want to scare her, especially when she clearly needed to relax and heal from whatever trauma he'd been unable to protect her from.

He'd had every intention to leave her alone in his bed to make her as comfortable as possible but when she'd asked him to stay, his weakness for her had won out.

The solar heat had lulled him to sleep but the few times he had woken up, the space between him and Verity had still been intact.

Which she had closed the distance sometime afterward.

Had she been conscious during the move or was she completely unaware of her actions?

Her hazel eyes blinked up at him. The sleep cleared from them instantly and she startled back, pressing her hands against his chest to propel herself away from him.

Knox lifted his arms, hands up to show that he wasn't keeping her against her will.

She sat up on the other side of the bed and kept her back to him.

He could hear her breathing heavily as her shoulders rose and fell quickly.

"It's okay," he said slowly. He wanted to reach out to her but suspected doing so would only freak her out more.

A few more moments passed before she finally calmed down enough to turn back around.

She held the blanket up to her chest like a shield and her eyes darted around the room, bouncing from his face, to his chest, to the door, ceiling, floor, and back again.

"I didn't—We didn't—What did—?"

"We slept together," Knox said. "Literally," he added. "I only woke up a moment before you did."

"I didn't mean to do...that." She gestured to his side of the bed, her cheeks flushing with embarrassment.

"Perhaps," he said, though he knew SOME part of her had driven her muscles to wrap around him. "But I didn't mind," he said.

"It's warm in here."

Stating the obvious, but Knox let her change the subject. "It concentrates solar energy and renews Eochronians as we sleep."

"Do I need sunlight to have energy now?"

Knox shrugged. "I don't know your percentage breakdown anymore, and you're manifesting in ways I didn't expect."

He hadn't meant to hurt her with his words but she tucked her chin into her chest and refused to meet his gaze.

"I really threw a wrench in your experiment, huh?"

"You're not an experiment to me, Verity," he said, shifting closer to her. "I thought you knew that by now."

"We haven't exactly had privacy for a heart-to-heart."

"And now that we do, you're hiding from me. I never knew you to be scared, Verity. Until I found you in that cell. What did Eiz'm do to you?"

She stiffened and squeezed her eyes shut as if doing so would erase whatever memory had reared its ugly head.

"Verity?"

"You already know," she murmured. "I tried to stop him—" her voice broke and tears started spilling from her eyes anew.

He stood and walked over to her side of the bed. Kneeling in front of her, he gently took her face in his hands and wiped her cheeks with his thumbs. "I'm sorry I wasn't here to protect you."

She nodded but didn't say anything else. She heaved another sigh. "I'm sorry—"

"Don't be sorry."

"I'm still tired," she continued. "Can I go back to sleep?"

"Of course," he said. "Take as much time as you need. I'll come back to check on you later."

This time, she didn't stop him from leaving. He closed the door to the bedroom and finally took off his armor, swapping it for his royal robes.

A refreshed Aerue, a shamefaced Arfilmea, and Dhaca were waiting. The latter two were wearing chains, and Knox was slightly surprised Aerue had actually imprisoned his sister for her crimes.

His ex-fiancée seemed pissed at the turn of events but the other guard didn't seem bothered by his position.

"I surrendered," Dhaca said by way of explanation. "I'm sorry, Your Majesty, for going against you. I know I must pay for my choice but I couldn't support him after what he did to her."

"You knew?" Knox bit out the words and resisted the urge to shout. He didn't want to wake Verity.

"I didn't know his intentions, Your Majesty. I swear. I only came in after and dressed her."

"You did nothing to help her."

Dhaca did nothing to defend himself.

Knox blew out a breath through his nose and forced himself to consider his options.

The guard had chosen to support Eiz'm's regicidal coup and turned against Aerue, his mentor, throwing him into jail to slowly die. Knox had no idea what else the man had done in his absence but he was sure there were other offenses on his roster. Perhaps he had threatened loyal council members and soldiers, or organized the Vruxol soldiers to attack Earth. All were severe crimes that could not go unpunished.

At the same time, Dhaca hadn't fought him, Aerue, and Verity. And though his actions were not nearly enough, he did show some kindness to the special human when Knox hadn't been able to do the job himself. That unselfish behavior should be rewarded in some way.

Arfilmea looked incredibly uncomfortable at Dhaca's discussion of the attack, and Knox turned his attention to her.

"What do you know?"

"What do you mean?"

"Don't play dumb, Arfilmea. It's unbecoming. You made your choices, now it's time to face the consequences. Including confessing your sins. Starting now."

"I saw her."

"When?"

"After."

"Dhaca?" he asked for confirmation.

"I saw her in the hallway but I can't confirm or deny what she knows about what Eiz'm had planned or what she did before, during, or after, Your Majesty."

She cut him a scathing look for ratting her out but Knox was certainly happy the man was accommodating his questions in his atonement.

He'd have to ask Verity if she'd seen his ex-fiancée but he had a feeling that both women had been aware of each other's presence.

Which meant Arfilmea had knowingly and purposefully refused to help her in her weakest moment. For that, she had to pay. But as much as he'd like to give Arfilmea capital punishment for her role in the uprising and not saving Verity from Eiz'm, he knew that Aerue would never forgive him. Which meant he needed alternative resolutions to both these traitors' cases that were severe enough without being tyrannical.

Then he'd have to worry about serving justice to his failure of a council and the surviving Eochronian soldiers on Earth. Perhaps he'd confiscate their armor and let them be handled by the human justice systems. They'd get probably many years in jail and he'd perhaps negotiate with Verity and her father to make sure they got some daily access to the sun but would otherwise leave the traitors to suffer. But if any of the human countries demanded the death penalty, he wouldn't intervene as the defectors deserved to pay for their crimes.

He'd command they not resist or escape but given how they'd already disobeyed him, he wasn't certain that would work. Hence the mostly sun-deprived isolation punishment he'd recommend to the humans.

Verity's father might hate him, but Knox knew the general wouldn't pass up the chance to exact some vengeance on the aliens who had attacked his planet and daughter.

Knox was also hopeful that his tenuous relationship with the man was improving based on his saving him from the fight and pursuing Verity to space. Of course, staying away after he'd killed Eiz'm was likely freaking the human out. But Verity needed rest and then Knox would return her as soon as possible.

She might have given into her subconscious desire of needing him for physical comfort but Knox wasn't naive enough to think that anything else had changed between them—from her perspective. And he wouldn't push her.

He had told the truth when he told her she was no longer an experiment and that meant he wasn't going to keep her as his prisoner again in the hopes of changing her mind about him.

Circumstances put into motion by her father had brought them together but Knox needed to end it. He'd never forget their short acquaintance for as long as he lived, however long that would be, but all good things must come to an end. And their relationship had certainly had its good share of negative parts.

Knox pulled himself from his thoughts and met Aerue's gaze over Arfilmea and Dhaca's heads.

"Aerue, place your sister in one of the prisoner cells and let it be known that anyone who provides her information or non-essential food will join her for disobeying their king." This whole ordeal proved he needed to start ruling with more consequences, and now was the perfect time to start. Arfilmea had attempted regicide and violated their sacred law of consent by not inter-vening on Verity's behalf while Eiz'm abused her. Her punish-ment would be paramount in setting a precedent for the other surviving traitors. "There will be no heating," which would prevent her from gaining too much energy for a jailbreak, "and she won't be fed."

Aerue's gaze hardened but he didn't object.

She made a sound of alarm but Knox ignored her.

"When she needs to regroup, she can contact you, and then you can escort her to the solarium."

His best friend nodded, wisely staying silent on his sister's case.

"Then come back and return Dhaca to his room. He will also be under house arrest with controlled his room heated at certain times when you are available to personally guard him." Knox didn't want to risk allowing him to travel even to the solarium, though it was becoming clear Dhaca had only been following orders, and not due truly believing Eiz'm's idealogy. Or, if he did, at the very least, he still respected their culture enough to stand against Eiz'm when he crossed the unforgivable line.

Knox might lift the sentence in the future, but he kept that possibility to himself.

If Knox had any other loyal soldiers left, he would have delegated more but Aerue was the only person left on the ship he implicitly trusted aside from Verity. Once Zeph and Trohm returned, he would instruct them to share Aerue's burden.

He supposed he trusted Dr. Mak'en but she wasn't in any position to become an armed guard. Besides, he needed to ask her about what work she wanted to do now that the experiment was done. If there were any human subjects left alive by Eiz'm, Knox would be sending them home with Verity.

He needed to check on that.

"Go now," Knox instructed Aerue.

His friend lifted his sister and they left together.

Knox didn't take his eyes off Dhaca but tapped out a message to the ship's tailors, instructing them to make sleeping clothes and a robe from the royal materials for Verity. They already had her measurements. She hadn't asked for new clothes but sleeping in her old human ones after what had happened to her likely irritated her skin, and the robe would provide her the privacy she'd clung to with his blanket.

Best case scenario, she used them for what they were intended. Worst case, she rejected the gifts.

He didn't dare hope she'd not only accept the clothes but also take them home with her as a memento of his caring for her.

"I really am sorry, Your Majesty," Dhaca repeated quietly.

Knox briefly closed his eyes before staring at him again. "I know you are." He didn't offer any hopeful words about reconciliation, however. He wasn't sure he would ever find it in him to forgive and trust the man enough. They would take the situation one day at a time.

Once Aerue returned and took Dhaca away, Knox poked his head back into the bedroom.

Verity was sound asleep.

He closed the door again and returned to the medical lab after securing his private suite so no one but him would be able to enter. It didn't prevent Verity from leaving the area if she wanted to but he highly doubted that would be happening in his short absence.

"Dr. Mak'en?" he called to get her attention.

She turned away from the data she was currently examining with a frown.

"What's wrong?"

"The humans seem to have maxed out their ability to assimilate our DNA."

Hadn't she told him the same thing last time he'd been on the ship?

"They're still alive?"

"I put them in comas and hid them before Eiz'm brought the Vruxols on board. But I was still tube-feeding them the treatment daily. Their numbers were good and they improved slightly since my last update to you. I wish they were viable enough to continue with the plan but I can't guarantee that with any certainty. Are you absolutely sure that Verity—"

"Is no longer an option," he finished. "But why do you think she took to it best?"

"She is female but she was also exposed to our DNA as a fetus. Her body likely never saw our treatment as an invasion to be fought off."

"Then why did she get sick?"

"The volume and speed of the transformation might have alerted her body's immune system because it was more than it was naturally exposed to." She made a gesture, and the data changed to show Verity's numbers again. "But her numbers continued increasing even while she was on Earth."

How did she know that?

"My sister was keeping me updated on her progress," the doctor said, answering his unspoken question.

"She was briefly taking the treatment in pill form," Knox said, avoiding directly discussing Dr. Makzik.

He wondered why Dr. Makzik had continued her sister's work on Earth if she had aligned with Eiz'm who believed the project was pointless but it probably had something to do with the experimental liquid she'd used to sedate him and the serum Eiz'm had attempted to give Verity before she'd turned it on him. If he had to guess, his rival had finished the plan he seemed to hate—though Knox wasn't sure why—and chosen a concentrated, intravenous administration over oral feeding.

"For how long and at what dosage?"

"Verity didn't exactly confide that information to me. And things got out of hand before your sister could tell me what dosage she had prescribed though I do believe it was more concentrated than what you were slipping into her food."

Dr. Mak'en nodded. "That could explain it, but again, her progress is still exponential compared to the others. But she's now at eighty-six percent."

Knox took a deep breath. He couldn't avoid this any more. "Dr. Mak'en, your sister attempted to kill me and I acted in self-defense…"

"But she's dead."

Her tone was remarkably flat, and Knox wondered what she was feeling in response to the news.

He nodded.

"Good riddance," Dr. Mak'en said, surprising him.

Had there been a sibling rivalry he was unaware of? They had seemed close every time he saw them together prior to Dr.

Makzik relocating to Earth. Perhaps Dr. Mak'en was secretly upset it hadn't been her?

Before he could say anything, she continued. "She made her choices, and aligning with Eiz'm was stupid."

He could have asked about the fact that she'd also made the serum for Eiz'm but as the doctor might have just done it for research purposes and not malicious ones, he was going to give the woman the benefit of the doubt.

Knox let the subject drop and leaned closer to the data. Verity had clearly blown the scientist's hypothesis that humans would max out at seventy-five but perhaps it was yet again due to her being a female or having the DNA grafted prenatally. Or both factors were partially responsible while their combined effect was greater than any of them would ever know.

Knox sighed. It seemed Verity was destined to stay a medical mystery as well as an emotional one. One he was running out of time to solve.

32

VERITY

VERITY WOKE with a start and kicked the blanket away. She felt like she was boiling, which was arguably better than the few times she'd woken up shivering since Knox had left her alone in the room.

Glancing around, he was clearly still gone.

Would he be coming back, or was he avoiding her after she'd accidentally wrapped herself around him like cling wrap? She wondered if he'd even say goodbye to her or if he'd fob her off on Aerue when she was finally ready to go back to Earth.

Why did the thought make her sad?

Shouldn't she be glad to get away from him for the last time and go back to her life? Because even if he followed her back to Earth and finished carrying out his plan, he had said that she wasn't an experiment anymore. Which meant he wouldn't be unexpectedly popping into her life, right?

And her father wouldn't let him near her again now that there was no reason for his help in defending the planet. If anything, her dad would label him an enemy again. Her feelings toward Knox were still incredibly complicated but she didn't want him to be hunted for the rest of her father's life. It would be a waste of her father's energy and unfair to the alien king after he saved her from Eiz'm and finally killed the bastard.

Verity started to close her eyes again when a flash of blue caught her attention near the door.

After confirming she was indeed alone, she scrambled out of bed and picked up the pile of blue clothes. It was the same shade as the dress she'd worn to her meal with Knox but these garments were a nightgown and a robe. Both felt cloud-soft and just as light. Much nicer than her current pajamas.

Verity closed her eyes and stripped then changed into the new wardrobe. She doubted Knox had surveillance in his own room but if he did, it wasn't as if he were seeing something new. Every time she changed as his prisoner had given him a peep show.

A small part of her wanted to ask him about it but she didn't want to spoil the silent truce they'd come to. There was no need to rock the boat.

She tried on the robe but then decided it would be too hot and refolded it before laying it on the pillow.

As if conjured by her thoughts, a knock sounded on the door before Knox poked his head in.

"You're awake," he said.

"You do know that entering immediately after knocking makes the warning gesture moot, right?"

He shrugged and fully entered the room, closing the door behind him. He leaned against the hard surface and crossed his arms. "How do you feel?"

She considered her answer as she rolled her neck, noting how his gaze followed her movement with banked heat.

"Better," she said. "But it's really hot in here."

"Sorry," he replied. "I forgot our body temperatures aren't the same."

"I didn't feel a difference—" she cut herself off. No need to bring up her hugging him in her sleep again.

He smiled and slowly approached the edge of the bed.

Verity watched as he lowered himself onto it and barely with-held the invitation to join her at the head of the mattress.

"I suppose there's less of a difference now that you have some Eochronian DNA but naturally, we run colder."

"Which is why you need sunlight," she said, echoing what he'd told her before about how his race generated energy. "So, you sleep like this all the time?"

He nodded.

"You never overheat?" How was that possible without an internal system for maintaining homeostasis?

"Not that I remember," Knox answered. "Though we do have sensors in the room that regulate the temperature." He tilted his head. "I didn't think to adjust it to account for your presence. I apologize."

Verity glanced down at the new nightgown, which left a lot more of her skin exposed and would keep her cooler than the pants and tank top. "I think I'll be okay," she said. She wasn't sure how much longer she'd be staying, anyway.

He gave her a quick once over and said, "I see the clothes fit you well."

His tone didn't give anything away but Verity found herself wanting him to compliment her sleepy appearance.

Knox wore similar sleep clothes but they were a deep burgundy instead of blue.

Together, they looked like a nebula. She'd seen images of space with more reds, yellows, and oranges—and even some green—but the blue, purples, and magenta, were always her favorite.

"Do you need to rest any more or would you be open to Dr. Mak'en examining you again before you go home?"

"Are you driving me back?" The question was out before she could stop herself.

Knox stilled and she regretted asking.

He turned toward her, searching her face so intently that she felt her cheeks heat.

"I was going to pre-program a pod to take you home but if you'd prefer to have an escort, I'm sure Aerue can accommodate you."

"But not you?" She had already shown her hand. What was the harm in digging her grave further?

He cleared his throat. "I suppose," he said. He stood and started pacing. "Though your planet may not welcome me."

"My dad will handle that."

Knox smiled.

"What?"

"I'm sure he would," he said, meeting her gaze before returning it to the floor in front of him. "He's expecting me to return you any moment now."

"You've talked to him?" She assumed he left out the part where she'd slept in his bed. Otherwise, he wouldn't be confident in her father backing his reentering Earth's atmosphere.

"I told him I'd bring you home safely. I haven't contacted him since I arrived back on my ship."

She let herself relax. It was completely irrational for her to worry about what her father would do if he knew the whole truth of her current situation but that hadn't stopped her from tensing up.

Knox kept walking, refusing to look at her again.

"Will you stop pacing?" she said. "You're making me dizzy." It wasn't strictly true but she was sick of him trying to avoid her from a few feet away.

He immediately halted and knelt at her side of the bed, taking her hand in his. "Should I call Dr. Mak'en in?"

She sighed. "I'm not that dizzy," she said. "I guess I'm still getting used to Eochronian speed. You used to hide it more around me."

"I hadn't considered you having a bad reaction," he said,

looking contrite. "I assumed with your improved speed it wouldn't be an issue."

"Not your fault. You've made it very clear that you have no idea why I'm reacting the way I am." Verity didn't say the words with any malice. She wasn't especially angry at him for it anymore, or her father. She was a freak of scientific experimentation but up until a month ago, her life had been normal and a good one. And both men clearly cared about her, even if they were both bad at showing it with healthy emotional communication like a normal person.

A shadow passed over his expression but cleared. He gave a rusty and forced chuckle. "I do apologize about that."

He stood and walked towards the door. "Now that you're awake, I'm going to have dinner set up in the sitting room. You can join me when you're ready."

Verity watched him leave and rubbed her temples. She was going to get a tension headache dealing with the alien king. At least one thing hadn't changed between them.

His private dining room hadn't been heated so she donned the robe and padded across the carpet to join Knox. He hadn't given her heels like he had for every other date, or even matching slippers, so she enjoyed the softness under her feet.

She found him cutting a platter of meat again.

A goblet full of the golden wine sat at both place settings and took her seat without waiting for him to pull the chair out.

A small frown pulled at the edges of his mouth.

"I didn't mean to rob you of a chance to be chivalrous," she said. "I can stand up if you want to push my seat in."

He waved her off but didn't offer another explanation for his reaction.

Verity watched as he plated the meat for each of them then took his own seat. She picked up her goblet and held it out to him.

He raised an eyebrow and murmured, "Still don't believe I'm not trying to poison you or slip you something special?"

She rolled her eyes. "Cheers, Knox," she said, "to defeating Eiz'm and you regaining your throne."

His glass met hers and they both took a sip.

He put his down first. "I technically never lost it."

"Sure," she said. "That's why your army attacked Earth against your orders."

He made a grumpy noise she'd expect from a small child, not a centuries-old alien king but she didn't tell him that.

"So," she said, "how many of these poor animals are still left for you to eat? Or have the two of us depleted the last of your supplies with all our dinner dates?"

"Dates, huh?"

"I just asked if I'm partially responsible for finishing off your kind's best and most luxurious source of nutrition and that's the part you focus on?"

He didn't answer other than to take another sip of his drink.

Verity did the same, noticing his eyes flare with heat again as she licked her lips clean of the golden nectar.

Such a guy.

Though she couldn't exactly throw stones. Watching his tongue flick out to do the same made her stomach tighten with heat.

She focused back on her plate and they ate in silence, each taking a second serving, until there was no food left in front of them.

Aside from the dessert on the side table, of course. But Verity was almost bursting with how full she was and wanted something else to top off the meal.

When he passed her to reach for the sweet cake, she grabbed his hand.

He stilled and looked at her, a question in his eyes.

"I'm not hungry for dessert," she said.

He nodded and sat back down across from her. "If you want more food, I can have the cook send up something else."

He wasn't understanding her.

"I'm not hungry for *food*," she said, emphasizing the last word, hoping that his spies on Earth had told him enough about this particular innuendo so she wouldn't have to spell it out for him.

His gaze slammed into hers and based on the heat lighting up his eyes like a supernova in his normally dark, galaxy irises was enough to knock the breath of her lungs.

He definitely understood her meaning.

"You're going to have to be very clear with what you want, Verity. Because if you're saying what I think you are—"

"I am," she said.

He strode to her in one smooth movement and pulled her out of her seat, pressing her soft body against his hard one. One hand kneaded her ass while the other branded her waist in a tender but strong grip that made it clear he wouldn't be releasing her until he was satisfied.

If she thought she had been breathless in reaction to his look, she had been wrong.

His hard erection pressed insistently against her hip as he pulled her close enough that she would be melting into him if physics weren't in the way.

It was the last thought she had before his mouth descended on hers, obliterating everything on her mind except how to feel more of him everywhere.

His hands rose from her body to cup her cheek and neck, tilting her head back to take more of his plundering kiss as his tongue swept inside and laying claim to all it touched.

There was barely any space between them, their chests pressed together so tightly that she could feel every small breath he took reverberate through her as if it were a vibrating motor, but Verity managed to snake her hands up his chest to his shoulders to steady herself.

She would have grabbed onto the lapels of his sleep jacket which should have given her player vibes but was too soft to make her feel sleazy. His shoulders were a better grip because she didn't want to wrinkle the material.

Though Knox didn't seem to share her concern, one of his hands had returned to her body, bunching the hem of her nightgown to slide it up her thighs.

She broke out in goosebumps and couldn't help the shiver that shook her frame.

It broke Knox out of whatever lustful haze he'd been wrapped up in since she'd given him the green light.

"Are you cold?" he asked against her mouth, as if he couldn't bear to move farther away from her even for a moment.

She shook her head. "No," she said. "But maybe we should move this away from the food?" She knew some people liked to get kinky with food but the idea never really appealed to her.

He didn't verbally respond but reached under her thighs and lifted her.

She took the silent cue to wrap her legs around his waist and clung to him as he walked them into his bedroom and lay her down on the bed.

He parted her legs with his thigh and ran a hand up and down her side but he didn't try to touch her anywhere else as they resumed kissing.

It was more heat than she'd ever experienced—even compared to their first kiss—but it wasn't enough. She shifted underneath him, trying to grind against him but he lifted his hips every time, refusing to give her the satisfaction she was seeking.

Maybe he was purposely torturing her, but a part of her knew he was trying to take things slow, and to not pressure her after what she'd already suffered.

When he gave her time to breathe again, she gulped in air and then held his face in her hands so she could speak.

"I'm okay, Knox." She kissed the corner of his mouth. "I'm

ready for more."

"Tell me if it becomes too much," he said, his voice rough with lust. "I need to know you'll stop me if you need to. I'll respect you no matter what happens."

She kissed the other side of his mouth then sucked his lower lip into her mouth, humming as she did so.

He groaned, and she lightly bit him.

His hands left her sides and moved to her waist, untying the robe, then moving up to her shoulders to push the fabric off.

She arched her back to help, and moaned when he kissed her collar bone before moving down the line between her breasts.

The nightgown didn't have nearly as deep a neckline as some of the dresses he'd given her before but it wasn't exactly modest either. He had plenty of room to play without having to shift the garment out of the way, and she had a feeling he would enjoy driving her out of her mind for as long as she'd let him.

She was right. He continued kissing all over her neck, chest, jawline, and even her temples, always switching his target just when she thought she couldn't take anymore of his tender caresses.

She groaned with impatience and he finally took pity on her, licking and sucking on her breast through the fabric.

Then the jerk bit her nipple, making her arch again.

"More," she whined.

He pressed his thigh more firmly between her legs and finally let her rub against him.

And then his hands slid down and finished his work from earlier, easing the nightgown up until the hem was at her waist, baring her to his hungry gaze.

He glanced up at her. "I've been dreaming about this since I met you," he said.

"Ditto," she whimpered, barely clinging to her sanity as a pleasurable pressure continued to build in her body.

"Can I taste you?" he asked.

She might combust if he didn't.

Verity nodded and he didn't waste any time in fulfilling his promise.

She gasped, arched, and clawed at his messy, dark hair as he kissed her there as thoroughly as he had her mouth.

Then his fingers joined in and she felt herself losing her mind all over again.

But while kept pushing her towards the edge, he repeatedly backed off before she could dive over.

Unable to take any more, she tugged on his hair until he lifted his head and met her gaze with a deliciously decadent one of his own.

"I need more," she said, pulling him up until they were face to face again.

He kissed her, and while he did, she made him catch up with her state of undress by pushing his jacket off with his help, and toyed with the waistband of his pants.

She barely touched his hard arousal before his hand covered hers.

"We don't have to," he said. "I don't need that from you."

"But I want to," she said. Logic demanded she also ask, "Will I get pregnant?"

Knox shook his head. "Eochronians can control whether we procreate during a coupling."

She groaned. That was *so* not fair.

"And this," he gestured between them, "isn't about that."

"Anymore," she said.

"Anymore," he echoed before kissing her again.

When she went to touch him, he let her this time, groaning and thrusting into her hand for more.

He pushed himself off her and discarded his pants before settling between her thighs again, this time, without anything separating them.

Panic seized her and she closed her eyes, trying to force

herself to relax.

Verity felt her world shifting and looked down at Knox when she opened her eyes.

He gave her a tender smile and tucked a strand of hair behind her ear. "Better?"

She nodded, leaned over, and kissed him, hoping to convey her gratitude.

When she came up for air, he asked, "Ready for more?"

She nodded and lowered herself onto him.

He maintained eye contact with her the whole time until she was fully seated on his lap, not straying once to glance at where their bodies joined.

Verity shifted again, still adjusting to his size. Seeing him naked that one time hadn't been enough to mentally prepare her but it wasn't painful like she'd worried. He'd turned her on so much that while she felt him *everywhere*, it didn't feel intrusive or anything other than perfect.

With one move, Knox sat up, bringing their foreheads together. "You're in control, Verity. Do whatever makes you feel good."

Given she'd only had two experiences before this, one good, one devastating, she wasn't exactly sure what to do but she rested her hands on his shoulders again and gave into her instinct to rock forward and backward.

From his drawn-out groan, she'd made a good choice. His hands went to her hips and held tightly but didn't try to control the movement.

He did, however, capture her mouth with his own and kissed her deeply again.

They briefly parted and he began trailing kisses down her jaw and neck again.

His return to her already sensitized skin drove her to start moving faster. But it wasn't enough.

Verity let out a groan of frustration and he chuckled before lightly biting her neck, sending another wave of pleasure through her.

"Knox," she whined, pulling at his hair. "More," she begged.

He pulled back and met her eye. "Are you sure?"

She nodded.

"I love you. You know that, right?"

She kissed him in answer.

Knox's hands tightened even more on her hips, holding her still as he started to thrust upward in tandem with every downstroke she made.

It was as if the chains on his self-control snapped because suddenly he was thrusting fast and furiously, his position on the bottom doing nothing to diminish his sexual power.

She could only wonder what it would feel like for him to be on top. The thought sent a shudder through her.

He'd been considerate to put her on top but now she wanted him to take charge.

She rested her hands on his chest and stopped moving.

He did too and looked up at her, a slightly confused expression tightening his features.

"I want you on top," she said.

"Are you sure?"

She nodded and found herself on her back a moment later.

"Hold on," he said.

There wasn't a bed frame to grab onto so she tangled her fingers in his hair and wrapped her legs around his waist again as he went to work on driving them both to climax.

When she finally exploded, Verity swore she saw stars shine in Knox's eyes but her eyes involuntarily closed before she could be sure.

He kept going until he, too, came and collapsed on top of her before turning so they both lay on their sides. His hand lightly gripped her hip, keeping her pressed against him.

Verity couldn't help but pant and wipe at her hair that now

clung to her face. How she had any energy left after their intense and prolonged lovemaking baffled her but she was now so hot in the room that she needed to remove the nightgown. If only she had enough energy to fully undress.

Knox was also covered in sweat but appeared to be shining iridescently like she'd seen him do with Arfilmea and even what she'd briefly seen in her mirror. Looking at her hand, she saw that it hadn't been a trick of the light after all. She had the same alien and multicolored appearance.

Knox trailed his hand from her neck down to her knee in a maddeningly gentle and leisurely fashion, already making her want to go for another round.

She laughed at the thought and he smiled.

"I love that sound," he said.

She couldn't help the smile spreading across her lips.

"That was…"

"I know," he said.

"Way to be modest."

"I was talking about you," he said, smiling back at her without any hint of sarcasm. "Now, let's rest before I take you back to Earth."

She didn't comment on how he'd changed his tune about her trip home but her heart felt light knowing that he wasn't going to send her off. Especially after what they had just shared.

"I really like you," she whispered. She wasn't going to lie and say the other L word when she wasn't sure but she could admit that she was more than merely infatuated with the alien king.

"I really like you, too," he said.

She could hear the smile in his voice.

"Now, go to sleep, Verity," he gently commanded, turning her around and spooning her from behind.

She resisted telling him that it was impossible to order someone to fall asleep. All the same, she closed her eyes and let herself bask in the warmth of his embrace.

33

KNOX

KNOX WATCHED Verity get dressed in her new wardrobe. He hadn't thought to order day clothes for her but his tailors had made them all the same. She now wore a loose blouse and pants that matched her sleep attire, which now lay in a rumpled pile at the end of the bed.

When they'd eventually woken up and made love again, he'd fully undressed her. An oversight on his part since she was absolutely beautiful in all her glory but he hadn't wanted to stop earlier.

Verity turned around and caught him watching her. She raised an eyebrow. "Something wrong?"

He shook his head. "Just thinking about you."

She took his hand and pulled him closer. "I'm right here."

"For a little while longer."

She looked almost sad at the reminder but didn't contradict him. They both knew it was the truth.

"Ready?" he asked, opening the door.

"Let's get this over with," Verity answered, leading the way to Dr. Mak'en's lab.

He supposed she'd been there enough times to have memorized the path but he was still impressed by the confidence with which she walked.

Dr. Mak'en wasn't immediately visible but Brauhm was. Knox greeted him then said, "Is she here?"

"She was just checking on the hu—remaining subjects."

The scientist had clearly stopped himself from obviously talking about the experiment, but Knox knew Verity probably caught the slip up all the same.

"Will they be going home?" she asked.

Knox nodded.

"Will they remember what happened to them?"

"We don't have memory wiping capabilities like you're imagining. They most likely will unless they experience post-traumatic amnesia."

She didn't answer and jumped up onto the examination table, swinging her legs impatiently.

Dr. Mak'en entered and quickly bowed upon seeing him.

"Doctor," he said, "we're getting ready to head back to Earth, and I know you wanted to examine Verity again before we departed."

"Of course, Your Majesty."

He didn't miss the way Verity rolled her eyes at his title, and he suppressed a smile at her dismissal. Despite everything between them, she still wasn't a fan monarchy—just as she'd said during their first meeting.

"Miss Landau," his scientist said, "lie down, if you please."

She did and waited while Dr. Mak'en scanned her with the same device as before.

The examination was much faster this time around.

"Everything seems in order."

"But?" Verity asked before he could.

"You are only fourteen percent human now. At this point, it would be very possible—"

"No," Knox cut in.

"Why not?" Verity asked.

He stared at her. "You'd give up the rest of your humanity? I already told you I don't see you as an asset to the experiment any more."

"It's not a huge percentage," she said.

"But enough that we don't know what it would do to you."

"Not different from this whole experience, then."

"Please give us a minute," he said, dismissing both Dr. Mak'en and Brauhm without sparing them a glance.

He waited until they were gone before he spoke again.

"What do you think you're doing?" he asked.

"You've already put so much work into this project, what's the problem with seeing it through to the end?"

"Because I don't want to experiment on you."

"Anymore."

Was he ever going to live that down? "Anymore," he said. "I love you as you are, Verity. I don't need you to change."

"But your kind is still depending on you to solve the population crisis."

"I'll find another way." He wasn't sure how, but he meant it.

She leaned forward and kissed him, surprising him.

When she pulled back, she rested her forehead on his and puffed out a laugh against his mouth. "You're being so stubborn. Just let me do this. Besides, I'll finally get to match you in your superpowers."

"I'm not a fictional character," he replied. He was losing ground. "And I don't want to put you in any more danger than I already have."

"Call them back in," Verity said.

"Think about what you're doing," he warned.

"Call them in, Knox."

He sighed and did as she asked.

Dr. Mak'en and Bruahm both entered, keeping their eyes down and avoiding his gaze.

"Against my wishes, Miss Landau has decided to proceed," he said.

No one said anything.

He looked up and saw them both staring at him anxiously, clearly unsure if they should go against him.

"Well?" Verity asked, cutting through the tension. "Are we going to do this or what?"

That snapped Dr. Mak'en out of her stunned stupor, and she gestured for Brauhm to step forward. In his hand was an applicator with the same red liquid Eiz'm had threatened Verity with during their final showdown.

Knox saw her flinch and said, "Stop."

Brauhm halted.

"No," Verity said. "Keep going. I'm okay."

Knox crossed his arms and watched as Brauhm placed the large, red adhesive to Verity's chest.

They all watched as the color faded to clear, the liquid being absorbed into her skin and leaving the container empty.

Dr. Mak'en scanned her brain and chest one last time. He saw the data revealing her numbers were now already past ninety despite just finishing the treatment. If it were happening that fast, she'd probably be completely Eochronian by the time they landed on Earth.

"How do you feel?" he asked her.

"Fine." She sat up and then wobbled. "Or, I was."

He turned to Dr. Mak'en for guidance on what was happening.

"She'll be okay, Your Majesty. But you may feel a little sick for the next few days as the transformation settles," she said to Verity.

What awful timing. He wanted to make sure she was okay, but once he'd brought her home to her father, he'd be leaving her behind. Permanently.

It occurred to him that Dr. Mak'en had probably intended to

broach the topic last night before he shut down the possibility of her continuing being in the experiment. He still didn't like it but had he known that the scientist also intended to ask Verity, about her feelings on the matter, and doing it earlier would have given him more time to take care of her.

Verity frowned at him, and he schooled his expression too late.

Knox ignored her and spoke into the communicator on his wrist. "Aerue, meet us in the hangar and prepare a pod for Verity and myself. Then send the others home, and recall Trohm and Zeph. Trohm will be your second-in-command."

He didn't bother to wait for his guard's affirmation before he turned his attention back to Verity, catching her forlorn expression.

Like he had before, she wiped her emotions away after he'd already seen them in full force.

"Ready to go?" he asked her.

She scooted off the exam table and slowly lowered her feet to the ground.

Knox resisted the urge to wrap his arm around her waist to help her. He needed to keep his hands to himself or he'd never let her go.

"Lead the way," she said.

"Thank you, Dr. Mak'en. Brauhm." Then he left the room and heard Verity follow.

Together, they walked to the hangar in silence.

Aerue was waiting for them.

"Arrow," she said, catching him off guard. He looked at his friend and raised his eyebrows. When had she given him a nickname?

Aerue didn't answer his silent question and instead addressed her. "Miss Landau, I hope you have a safe trip."

"Thank you. I'm not steering, though, so I think we'll be fine."

Aerue nodded but didn't offer a further comment.

Knox grabbed her elbow and steered her towards his ship.

Resting a hand on the side, he unlocked the door and waved her inside.

She took the passenger seat next to his, and he closed the door behind them.

He felt her gaze on him as he performed the flight security check and input the navigational data to the airbase instead of over the state border where he'd last landed.

Knox expected her to say something about going home, but she remained silent while buckling herself in. Then he put the pod into drive and left his home ship behind.

He turned and saw her sitting stiffly in her seat, her gaze resolutely on the planets and stars outside the window.

Perhaps she was still adjusting to the treatment. If it were something else, he was sure she'd tell him. She'd never shied away from being brutally honest and blunt with him about anything. Why would now be any different?

True, he'd confessed his love for her and she hadn't returned it, but they were parting on good terms.

A part of him wished they weren't, but he couldn't go back on his decision to leave her life now. If she wanted him to stay, she would have already told him, and she hadn't.

He gripped the steering mechanism tightly and pushed the thought out of his mind.

He'd stick to the plan and cherish the memories he had with her for as long as he lived. But that would be the end of it.

34

VERITY

VERITY WATCHED the night sky speed past them, even though she knew in reality they were the ones moving through space at a blistering pace. Unlike last time, she wasn't as dizzy because she could differentiate the stars better than a single blur of light.

Probably an effect of becoming more alien just like her new speed and strength. Honestly, she now had almost every power associated with fictional vampires aside from thirsting for blood. Was it possible that Knox's moles had inspired the mythology?

She opened her mouth to ask, then shut it. She crossed her arms and refused to look at Knox, who had barely kept eye contact with her longer than a second after she'd decided to become fully like him. After everything he'd done, he seemed almost angry at her choice.

Well, tough shit.

And it was too late to go back now, anyway.

She wasn't dizzy anymore but she could almost feel herself changing as she sat in the passenger seat.

Maybe he wasn't freezing her out because of that, though.

She had to admit the very real possibility that he was hurt she hadn't returned his "I love you," and was protecting himself.

Verity didn't think he was trying to punish her for not sharing his feelings. For all his domineering attitude, some of which was merely by virtue of him being a king and leader of an army, he had never actively tried to hurt her.

Before long, her blue and green planet appeared before them.

"You might want to announce yourself," she said. "Would suck to be shot out of the sky."

His lips quirked in a smile. "We'd be fine, but if it makes you feel better." He touched the same button she had on the ceiling of the pod when she'd escaped home, and spoke, "This is Knox arriving with Verity Landau, daughter of General Landau."

He motioned for her to talk with his other hand before returning it to the steering mechanism.

"Hello," she said. "This is Verity. We should be landing soon. Please stand all weapons down. Talk to my father if you have to."

When she didn't add anything else, he released the button and resumed the cold shoulder act.

Verity rolled her eyes and leaned further back in her seat.

A few moments later, they had entered the atmosphere and the light blue summer sky surrounded them. The enemy ships had clearly disappeared sometime during her stay in space.

Knox guided them to land outside the base. Before she could do it herself, he unbuckled her and ushered her out of the pod.

She almost dug her heels in just to prolong their time together. Which was stupid since she still wasn't sure if she was in love with him or not. Having sex didn't always mean love and commitment—a lot of her friends had proven that time and again —but it wasn't a purely physical connection either.

She mentally cursed herself for her indecision. But she refused to say something she wasn't able to fully back.

Inside the checkpoint, her father greeted her the same way he had when she'd come back with Ben and Zeph.

He ran to her and engulfed her in a bear hug that had her almost toppling backward.

She grabbed onto him and patted his back. "I'm okay, Dad." A lie if she considered everything Eiz'm had done to her, but watching Knox had definitely helped a little. But an understatement if she took into account she was now fully Eochronian and therefore stronger than any human, including her father.

"What took you so long to come back?"

"Knox's doctor had to fix me up." She left out the part where that had actually only taken a few minutes and the rest of her time had been spent in Knox's company, especially in his bed.

She heard Knox approach from behind but didn't acknowledge her. Instead, she watched him hold out his hand to shake her father's.

To her surprise, her dad returned the gesture without hesitation and she saw a glimmer of respect in his eyes.

"I'll be taking my leave now," the alien king said. "I wish you all the best, General Landau. Miss Landau."

His formality made her want to smack him.

Her father must have seen her anger because he took a step back and cleared his throat. "I'll be in my office when you're done," he said before walking away, leaving her alone with Knox.

She turned to him and saw he was staring at her father's retreating back with a bemused expression on his face.

"That's it?" she demanded.

He finally looked at her. "That's what?"

"We sleep together, you say you love me, then you barely talk to me and are dropping me off without a goodbye?"

"I wished you well. Doesn't that count as a farewell?"

"Don't be a smart-ass. You were addressing my dad and couldn't completely ignore me in front of him without him asking questions." She took a deep breath and tried to reign in her hurt anger. "Are you upset that I didn't say 'I love you' back?"

She felt weak for asking but she just had to know.

His expression shuttered. "No."

"That's it?" She was getting really tired of his non-answers.

"I'm not upset, Verity. I understand you don't return my feelings. We certainly didn't meet under circumstances that would lend themselves to you, so I can't be disappointed."

He sounded so detached and clinical. She hated it.

"I don't know what I feel, Knox," she murmured.

He gave her a sad smile.

"I suppose it's for the best. I really want you to have a good life, Verity."

"But I'm now fully Eochronian." She didn't have a test saying it but she knew it to be true deep in her soul. "What if I need to ask you questions about it?"

He pulled something out of his jacket and handed it to her. "You can always contact me through this."

She read the device's markings and saw pretty simple instructions. "I'm going to guess this isn't in English and I'm just reading it naturally."

He nodded.

She pocketed it and waited for him to say something else.

When he didn't, she took a step closer to him. "This can't be it," she whispered.

"While your father might no longer want to kill me on sight, I'm not exactly welcome on Earth."

"But what about your kind? You were planning on settling here."

"I'll find another way. You don't need to worry about my problems, Verity."

"But–"

"You never needed to." He took a step back. "I have to go now." She thought she heard him add, "or I never will" under his breath but wasn't totally sure.

"I don't think it's a bad plan," she said. "Now that we know you exist, you don't have to do it through deception."

A playful light entered his eyes. "Are you offering?"

She couldn't stop the blush that heated her cheeks.

"If I stayed…" he tilted his head examining her, "would you be open to… being in a relationship with me?"

She nodded without hesitation. Her father and therapist would probably think she was crazy but they weren't here right now and she wasn't going to lie to Knox or herself.

"I assume it's too early to ask you to become my queen, too?"

"You'd be correct. Besides, I may be fully Eochronian now but I don't think your kind will like me as a ruler. And Earth isn't going to acknowledge us as planet-wide royalty."

"My people would respect you." He had no doubt in his voice. "And Earth could see it as a valuable alliance."

He had a point but they were getting ahead of themselves.

"So, will you stay?"

"I need to go back right now," he said. "But I can visit if you want me to."

"I want you to." She glanced over her shoulder to make sure there weren't any guards watching them who might report back to her father. Satisfied they were all looking somewhere else, she planted a quick peck on Knox's lips and enjoyed the surprised look on his face. "Now, go be king of space."

"I'm not that grand."

She smiled. "You know what I mean."

He kissed her then pulled back. "I'll see you soon, Verity."

She watched him walk back to his ship, disappear behind the door, and rise into the sky.

When she could no longer see him, she turned and walked towards her father's office where he was waiting for her. She was glad to be home without the threat of being kidnapped or tortured, but she also already couldn't wait to see Knox again.

EPILOGUE

One Month Later

KNOX RAISED his hand and knocked on the door.

A moment passed before Verity's father opened it.

"Is she here?"

"She's currently at an appointment but she should be back soon." The man stepped back to let him in. "How are things?"

"Good," he replied.

The month had been a busy one with very little time for anything other than restructuring his council to diminish their power and rewarding his agents who had remained faithful to him on Earth.

He had decided to recall all the traitors from Earth. They were individually being tried by the triumvirate of Aerue, Trohm, and Zeph. He trusted them to make a recommendation for each of the offending individuals.

A few of the other traitors had already been executed. The threat of losing their lives had made every remaining turncoat nervous about their future.

Knox hadn't visited Arfilmea once, and even Aerue hadn't

bargained on her behalf after that first day upon his return from dropping Verity home. The plea had been to let her live under house arrest with limited solar exposure like Dhaca instead of leaving her in the ship's bowels to languish in absolute isolation and no energy source.

Trohm and Zeph had both voted for her to be put to death in a public ceremony, but she was still the sister of his best friend and ally. Knox couldn't bring himself to order her killed in a swift punishment, though one could argue a lifetime of wasting away was worse.

His decision dragged out her sentence but it also felt more appropriate given her involvement in the conspiracy and coup against him. Her crimes against Verity, which had been further explained to him by Dhaca, made it only fair that she be imprisoned like Verity had been by Eiz'm since Knox wouldn't condone anyone committing the same atrocities against her—even if it were in the name of just retribution.

Rumors of her suffering had spread like wildfire, aided by Trohm's loud mouth in disseminating the news, and some traitors came forward like Dhaca to express remorse.

Knox wasn't sure he believed them as much as he did the former guard but they were still better than the ones who refused to beg forgiveness of him. He couldn't tell if it was pride or the misplaced belief Eiz'm would have been a better leader even after they had all vehemently disavowed Eiz'm's violating another's consent. It was their most sacred law and while many still saw humans as inferior—an opinion Knox doubted he'd ever be able to fully overturn—no one had attempted to defend Eiz'm's worst and final crime.

Knox was surprised Arfilmea hadn't yet died but the time was fast approaching. He'd allow Aerue to observe the customary mourning traditions but he wouldn't, nor would anyone else. She had been the once future queen but her choices had sealed her fate and she would not be remembered as a martyr.

But he wasn't on Earth to discuss the Eochronian state of affairs with General Landau. He was there to check in on Verity. From what she'd told him in their few communications since he last saw her, she still hadn't told her father that she was no longer human but the general was too intelligent to not realize she had changed again during her second abduction.

Knox watched the human general disappear upstairs then sat in the living room on the leather armchair and waited for her to appear.

He could make out her talking to a woman—her therapist—across the base, but he withdrew his hearing to give her privacy.

Fifteen minutes later, the front door flew open and she appeared in the threshold.

"Knox," she greeted, a smile gracing her lips.

He stood and catalogued her appearance. Her eyes now resembled a bluish-purple galaxy and sparkled in contrast to her bronze, sun-kissed skin. "You look well."

"Thank you."

He watched her gaze quickly shift to the doorway before back to him.

"Your father is upstairs," Knox said, even though he suspected she heard the footsteps as clearly as he did.

She leaned in and kissed him.

He held in the groan that threatened to escape when her fingers tunneled through his hair and pulled him closer to her height. After everything, she still remained petite.

Knox placed his hands on her hips and pushed lightly, forcing her to break the kiss.

She looked up at him and he spoke at a sub-audible frequency. "Not with your father home."

"Then take me somewhere else."

He raised his voice loud enough for her father to hear. "We're going out for a bit, General. She'll be back soon."

"Not too soon, I hope," she muttered.

He grabbed her hand and ran with her back to his ship.

It was still much smaller than the mothership but he had expanded and renovated it to include a bedroom suite for this very scenario as his undercover agents had given up their human housing.

If things continued to go well, however, maybe he'd consider buying a home on the planet so he and Verity could spend time together in a more welcoming and permanent location.

———

VERITY TOOK in the updated ship and couldn't help but smile at the added bed.

It was smaller than the one they'd shared during their love-making but looked just as comfortable and left more than enough room for them to have an encore.

She watched Knox shut the pod's entrance, ensconcing them in a personal bubble protected from the outside world.

He met her gaze with a heated one of his own and she stared unabashedly as he started to disrobe.

A part of her wanted him to undress her but she was also too impatient to waste time on that so she stripped quickly and lay down on the bed.

His eyes flared as he joined her on the mattress, his knee spreading her open.

Knox kissed her deeply while his fingers coasted over her body then entered her.

She arched her back and he began preparing her by lazily thrusting his digits in and out while his thumb teased her clit.

He must have been as impatient as her because as soon as they could hear her wetness, he removed his hand and fitted his cock at her entrance and slid in deep, kissing her again to swallow her gasp of pleasure at the fullness. How many times had she gone to bed remembering how good it felt? But recreating it by herself paled in comparison to the real thing.

Lust was already clouding her mind but while she could still think clearly enough, she tugged at his hair until he ended the kiss. "You said we can control if we want to procreate?"

His gaze sharpened and roamed her face. "I did."

"I love you, Knox." She rolled her hips to take him deeper, earning a grunt from him. "And I want to have a future with you."

"I love you, too." He kissed her forehead, then rested his own against hers and let their breaths mingle as they continued moving in unison. "Will you marry me and become my queen?"

"You asked me that before."

"Mmhm." He thrust particularly hard, making her actually mewl. "And I want to hear an answer. Even if it's the same as last time. Though I hope it isn't." His last words were whispered against her mouth and she shivered.

"If you propose to me more romantically..." she teased.

Amusement lit his gaze. "I can, if you need me, too, but I think we're past that. Don't you?"

"Ask me again," she said.

He chuckled and humored her. "Verity Landau, will you marry me and become not just the mother of my child but also my wife and queen?"

She cradled his face in her hands. "Yes, Knox, king of the Eochronians, I will." She kissed him briefly but didn't let him deepen it yet. "Now, make love to me please?" They were going to have to tell her father and it would go much better if they were both satisfied and able to focus on keeping their hands off each other when they did.

"With pleasure." He claimed her mouth, body, and soul as he consumed her and made good on her request.

Verity closed her eyes and gave herself over to the rhythm. When she finally came, she clenched around him and bit his lip. He began pounding her faster than before and she felt him explode inside her, filling her with warmth. She wrapped her thighs around his waist and held tight as he then gentled his pace and finally withdrew.

He kissed her again, tenderly cherishing her. She returned the gesture, silently pouring her love into him as they lay together.

"I love you, Knox."

"I love you, too, Verity."

"Now we just have to tell my dad."

Her future husband groaned against her mouth but it sounded more pained than lustful this time. He lifted his gaze to meet hers. "A small price to pay for a prize as precious as you."

She smiled. "Just remember that when he vows to kill you if you don't make me happy."

"I will." He gave her a peck on the lips. "And since I plan to keep you happy for the rest of our very long lives, I'm not concerned by that threat."

"Good," she said, sitting up. "Then we should get it over with. Because once we get his approval, I want to come back here and get started on our happily ever after."

"We already have," Knox said. "The moment you agreed to marry me."

He kissed her, pulling her down again, making her laugh.

She surrendered to his amorous ministrations.

Telling her father could wait.

ALIEN PRONUNCIATION GUIDE

Verity - Ver-i-tee

Eochron - ee-yo-kron
Eochronian - ee-yo-crone-ian

Vruxol - vr-ux-ull
Vruxilian - vr-ux-ill-ian

Lielneh - Leel-neh

Aerue - aye-rue
Arfilmea - ar-fil-me-ah
Eiz'm - eyes-um
Knox - nox
Trohm - tro-m

AUTHOR'S NOTE

Important note: authors live on reviews. And so, I ask you, my wonderful reader, to leave a review on your favorite retailer, and recommend this book to your friends.

If you would like a free book and to be kept in the loop about all my future publishing endeavors, subscribe to my newsletter at www.zarahoffman.com/subscribe

ACKNOWLEDGMENTS

As always, thank you so much to my readers. I couldn't do this without you.

I also want to give a special shoutout to my *viewers*. This was the first story I talked about on my YouTube channel and the excitement I got from my subscribers really helped me stay motivated as I worked on it in the crazy quarantine and lockdown periods of 2020.

I'd like to thank my cover designer, Alivia Anders of White Rabbit Book Design for the gorgeous cover. I cannot tell you how many people have complimented it.

Thank you to all my early readers who helped make this story the best it could be: Dania, Hannah, Maria, and Regina.

ABOUT THE AUTHOR

Zara Hoffman is a graduate student in the NYU Masters in Publishing Program and has been writing since she was eight years old. She spends most of her time doing homework and writing new stories because if she didn't, her head would likely explode. Her books are for young adults or the young at heart. After all, growing up is overrated.

www.zarahoffman.com
zarahoffman@zarahoffman.com

ALSO BY ZARA HOFFMAN

The Belgrave Legacy

The Belgrave Legacy

Unmoored

Taming the Alpha

Stellar Blood

Obscure Origin

Bitter Blood